PRE - COLUMBIAN MEXICO PLANS, PITFALLS, AND PERILS

A FICTIONAL - HISTORICAL NARRATIVE

Mark J. Curran

 **www.trafford.com**

North America & international
toll-free: 844-688-6899 (USA & Canada)
fax: 812 355 4082

DEDICATION

To Keah who joined the author on Pre – Columbian
travels, but that's another story.

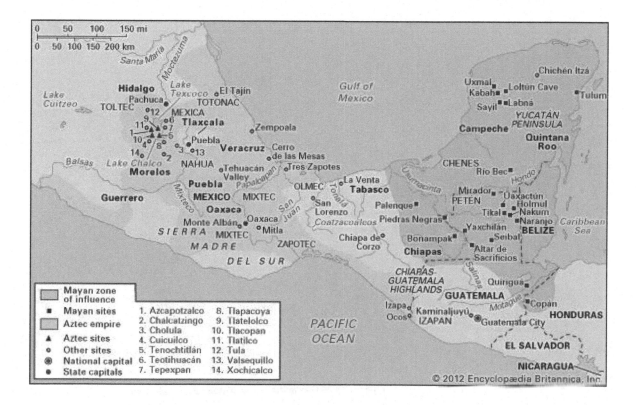

0 50 100 150 mi
0 50 100 150 200 km

Santa María

Lake Cuitzeo

Hidalgo
Pachuca
TOLTEC
○12
11 ○ ○8
○7
1 ▲▲○
10○ ▲○5
4○ ○8
14○ ○2
NAHUA
Morelos

Lake Texcoco
MEXICA
Tlaxcala
El Tajín
TOTONAC

Balsas

Lake Chalco

▲○ Puebla
○13
Veracruz
Zempoala
Cerro de las Mesas
Tres Zapotes

Tehuacán Valley

Papaloapan

Gulf of Mexico

Puebla
MEXICO **MIXTEC**

Guerrero

Oaxaca

Monte Albán ■
MIXTEC

SIERRA

MADRE

DEL SUR

Oaxaca○ ○Mitla
ZAPOTEC

OLMEC
San Juan

San Lorenzo
Coatzacualcos

Tonalá

La Venta ■
Tabasco

Palenque ■

Chiapa de Corzo ○

Chiapas

CHIAPAS GUATEMALA HIGHLANDS

Uxmal ■
Kabah ■
Sayil ■
○ Chichén Itzá
Loltún Cave ■
■ Labná
Tulum
YUCATÁN PENINSULA

Campeche

Quintana Roo

CHENES
Río Bec ■
Hondo

Mirador ■
PETEN
Tikal ■
Oxactún ■
Holmul ■
Nakum ■
Naranjo ■
Piedras Negras ■
Yaxchilán ■
BELIZE

Bonampak ■
Seibal ■
Altar de Sacrificios ■

Caribbean Sea

Quiriguá ○
Salinas

Motagua
Copán ○
HONDURAS

GUATEMALA

Izapa○
Ocos○
Kaminaljuyú ○
IZAPAN
Guatemala City ◉

EL SALVADOR

PACIFIC OCEAN

NICARAGUA

□ Mayan zone of influence
■ Mayan sites
□ Aztec empire
▲ Aztec sites
○ Other sites
◉ National capital
● State capitals

1. Azcapotzalco
2. Chalcatzingo
3. Cholula
4. Cuicuilco
5. Tenochtitlán
6. Teotihuacán
7. Tepexpan

8. Tlapacoya
9. Tlatelolco
10. Tlacopan
11. Tlatilco
12. Tula
13. Valsequillo
14. Xochicalco

© 2012 Encyclopædia Britannica, Inc.

PROLOGUE

It's 1973 and I'm in Lincoln at the University of Nebraska doing a job I love but always looking ahead. If you've read my now several books you know the whole story, but that makes you a very rare bird. In the world of Piliated Woodpeckers or Arara - Coara Toucans, my crowd would be Western Meadowlarks or maybe Sand Hill Cranes out on the Platte. Oh, where was I? Wheat, alfalfa and cornfields can get to you after a while. For the multitude unfamiliar with goings on the last three years, here's an update.

I'm Mike Gaherty, an Assistant Professor with Tenure at the University of Nebraska in Lincoln. For academic denizens that says it all. It means I've got a good job, am working at a decent if not a nationally recognized university whose name is on the tip of everyone's tongue, but like Garth Brooks says in "I've Got Friends in Low Places," "I'm okay." I teach Spanish and Portuguese (Brazilian variant, thank you) languages and their respective cultures. So, you see I'm not a literary theory or egghead scientist or techno - business guru and that will make a lot more sense as we move along.

In Spanish I'm trained in the Literature of Spain, mainly Golden Age Literature, so we could talk about Lope de Vega and Calderón de la Barca in the Drama, Garcilaso de la Vega or Luís de Góngora in the poetry, and mainly Miguel de Cervantes's "Don Quixote de la Mancha." There's a smattering of experience and love for 20th century novelists in Latin America, mainly Carlos Fuentes' sagas of Mexico. That's because I studied several years ago at Mexico's National University in D.F. and went on to travel in Guatemala, my introductions to Pre – Columbian Cultures.

Because I had no big bright ideas on publishing in Spanish Literature (or the chance to teach such courses because there was a "lock-down" on them by insecure, nervous Spanish colleagues) my ticket to tenure was Brazil and a really fortuitous find in its folk – popular literature in verse or as most call it, "A Literatura de Cordel." It sounds a bit esoteric but it ain't! "Cordel" happens to be written in verse by humble poets from the backlands and coastal cities of Northeastern Brazil, but its literally a couple of hundred thousand chapbook style titles - booklets not only entertain and teach but are the "newspaper" for the poor masses of Brazil. And more – it really tells the history of all Brazil in the 20th century. That brings me back to recent times.

After two great experiences in continued research in Brazil in the summers of 1971 and 1972 with good results for writing and tenure, there are now three books of "Letters from Brazil" sponsored by the "New York Times" and facilitated by James Hansen, head of the International Section of the "Times" and instrumental in publication by their press. In addition, there is a book and articles published on the "Cordel" and Brazilian Literature in academic circles in Brazil. That's what got me tenure and promotion. The bad news is I can't go back to Brazil for the immediate future due to what I have written about the military government's censorship vis a vis Brazil's best-known composer and singer of very sophisticated "samba," Chico Buarque de Hollanda. The General at the censorship board put it best: "We are not throwing you out of Brazil but are inviting you to get on tomorrow's flight to New York." I was however able to get back to my beloved Brazil last summer, but not as a scholar; there was a surprise invitation as cultural lecturer for Adventure Travel on their "International Adventurer" Expedition Ship. And I met a terrific girl, really a soul-mate, on the trip; she was "Assistant Adventure Leader" setting up all on - shore travel in Brazil this last summer of 1972. That leads me now to the present and this narration.

The idea of a return to Mexico and Guatemala with a short jaunt to Copán in Honduras and a new "Letters" was a suggestion to James Hansen a year ago when Brazil no longer seemed to be an option. Now it is joined in another venture to investigate and sound out an itinerary for a new trip by Adventure Travel (expeditions on land and not on the sea) to the same area. I'm hatching all this in the Fall Term of 1972 and if all goes well, doing the return the summer of 1974.

1

JAMES HANSEN'S APPROVAL

Prior to travel and what evolved there was a lengthy phone call to James Hansen at the "Times," first to apprise him of my idea and then after some hesitation and I daresay, negotiation, garner his tentative approval and go ahead with the early planning phase of the project. There was a lot of water under the bridge and events regarding yours truly Mike Gaherty that he did not know – the unexpected "gig" for Adventure Travel and the role as cultural speaker for the trip around Brazil on the "International Adventurer" in the summer of 1972. He was happy to hear from me, as always, and surprised about the 1972 trip, wondering how all that had happened vis a vis my rapid exit from Brazil in 1971 and the events reported in "Letters III." I filled him in and promised I would send him the account of the whole thing, the book written now in the Fall and Winter of 1972 – 1973 – "Around Brazil on the 'International Explorer' A Fictional Panegyric."

"Mike, you know I appreciate and love your writing; the series of 'Letters from Brazil,' albeit not a best – seller, has provided interesting and even provocative reading for the 'International Section' diehards of the 'Times.' I was tempted by the way to edit out the amorous adventures, but once again, we wanted 'the full story;' so be it. I guess I should not be surprised at your latest; your job and tenure at Nebraska might lend to a desire to get away! Ha ha. So, my friend from out west, what's cooking?"

1

"James, perhaps you remember that last conversation in New York in 1971 and my 'brainstorm' of doing something different if or until things should change in Brazil. I mean the idea of 'Letters from the Pre-Columbian world in Mexico and Mesoamerica.' That's what this is all about. The project has not exactly 'jelled' but the brain is whirring and the wheels turning, albeit with a couple of twists. I'm thinking of some extended travel back to Mexico, Guatemala and a short jaunt into Honduras at Copán for a report on that fascinating part of the world. I've xeroxed a tentative outline of the topics of interest and will mail it to you right away so you can see the scope of the thing. I know you have a sub-division of NYT Travel and you mentioned your excellent connections to the National Geographic Society, but I'm not thinking of anything so fancy. It would be a return to the 'Letters' format, sending you a letter – essay every couple of weeks with what I have seen, in this case, a geographic, cultural overview of Pre – Columbian Civilization in Mexico and Mesoamerica. You may remember I teach Spanish as well as Brazilian Portuguese, have studied and traveled in the area, and have taught much of it in the Spanish American Civilization Class at Nebraska. What you do not know is that the level of enthusiasm is almost up to that of Brazil.

"I'm no archeologist or anthropologist or decipherer of glyphs, but I'm capable of writing an interesting overview with travel experiences, and as always the connection to cultural, political and religious happenings along the way. Your readers would have a broad, current view of the area and its possibilities for travel. Travel – that's where the second part of my proposal comes. Adventure Travel in Los Angeles really liked my work last year and wants me to sign on for their next trip to Brazil. Well and good and I'm happy, but am not ready to go back so soon (they agree; you have to space out the experiences and get new customers). But I did propose this Mexico – Mesoamerica idea to them and they perhaps surprisingly said they were looking into adventure travel possibilities other than by sea. In short, they are willing to pay me a stipend and travel expenses for the initial research during the summer months of this next year 1973. I'll not miss any time at Nebraska and can get back to an old love. Oh, love, there is a matter related to that, or at least 'mutual admiration;' my partner in the research would be their 'girl wonder' Amy Carrier with degrees from Cornell in Hotel Management and advanced study at the Fundação Getúlio Vargas in Rio for Business in that country (she worked for Marriott International for two years prior to working with AT). We worked together on the ship last year, made a good team, so I've requested AT personnel for her to accompany me for something I sure can't do – check out high end lodging for the prospective customers. AT said yes and so did Amy, so she will be coming along. The rub I know is you can't mix NYT Travel with this company, although not a strict competitor at least up to the present. But I think you can perhaps welcome the 'Letters.' So what do you think?"

"Mike, there are a couple of issues and you might not be too comfortable with what I have to say, but we've known each other and worked together now for over three years with excellent results. First, Mike, we've already talked about your writing and results from Brazil, but if I'm not wrong, there's a big difference between that and the Pre-Columbian issue. What can you tell me about that?"

"Mr. Hansen, James, correct, the time spent either in Mexico or Central America does not compare to the total time and dedication to Brazil. Here are the facts: I did live in Mexico City for a few months over ten years ago while studying at the National University [UNAM] and did travel to Guatemala. More important, I did in – depth study of the area in the Ph.D. program in Spanish at Georgetown and am quite confident that the knowledge I have is correct and interesting. And I taught the subject matter in civilization courses at U. of N. Finally, I am sure I can write an equally informative and entertaining 'Letter' from Mexico and Guatemala."

"Mike, that makes me feel better on the first count. In regard to mixing NYT Travel and AT you are right about that, and I'm not sure how you can write a new series of 'Letters' and leave Amy and travel research and logistics out. And I would face a conflict of interest publishing the 'Letters' if AT is mentioned. Send me your outline. It occurs to me that the 'Times' has many faces and facets and if your trip and AT research worked out, it could be feasible to combine, a one-time thing, NYT Travel and AT Travel for the one trip (it's done all the time in the travel market). Business is business and if it means more customers for each of us, and the business is competitive and even cut – throat. I don't think anyone will argue.

"If I understand you, this is a big experiment on their part, land expedition travel, and they might welcome a boost of potential travelers from us. We are not exactly fly – by – night, so it might work both ways. I think the business people call it 'a joint venture.' Ha! We already have trips all over the world, but not our own fleet of ships or AT's oceanic expertise. And for that matter National Geographic won't be displeased; they have cut way back on full-time photographers and are requesting much more free -lance work, so if this should in any way provide short stints of work for the free – lancers, all would be happy. I'm not saying you need photographers to come along on your research trip, but both NYT and AT will be sure to want them on the actual expeditions should they come to pass. Send that plan post-haste, give me a week to make some calls, and I'll get back to you in about two weeks."

It does indeed work both ways, I apprised Susan Gillian in Personnel at AT and Amy of the proposal of new "Letters" to James Hansen, his openness to a possible "joint venture," gave him Susan's phone number, so sat on pins and needles for two weeks seeing what might surface, as it were. And it did as I'll tell.

2

AMY IN DENVER AND ADVENTURE TRAVEL IN LOS ANGELES

I'm getting ready to go to the airport in Omaha, catch a flight to Denver and from there to Los Angeles. Why Denver? That's where Amy Carrier is currently visiting her parents, between assignments for AT. It's a chance for a reunion and some strategy before we meet with her supervisor and managers at AT later in the week. We have the green light from James Hansen in New York to pursue the Mexico idea and the joint venture with NYT Travel and AT. It's March, a good time to get out of Lincoln for a while, actually spring break, so the campus empties like a NYC subway stop, students and faculty heading anywhere it's warmer. I'm a bit nervous to meet her parents; if you grew up in my generation, going to a girl friend's parents' house in another city, being introduced and on top of that, bunking in one of the guest rooms, is a sign of things to come. There's no engagement, far from it, we really don't know each other that well, but there's great friendship and excitement for what's to come.

That's where I can fill in some blanks. James Hansen and AT bigwigs have been on the phone and agreed to sponsor and share the expenses of a fact – finding research trip for Mexico and Mesoamerica. Amy and I are going to Los Angeles to iron out the details. AT's trip planner, James

Morrison, and Susan Gillian are both in on it and we'll meet at the offices on Wilshire close to UCLA for planning and some negotiating I surmise. I've got xeroxes of my plan for Amy and James, and she has been using her travel agent contacts for initial information on flights, hotels and tourist sites for Mexico, Guatemala and Honduras. We'll match up ideas for itinerary and serious work can start next week.

Back to Denver. Amy met me out at Stapleton and was a sight to see as I came out of the walkway from the plane. Pretty as ever, looking good, a big smile on her face. We kissed and hugged and were basically just doing catching up stuff as we waited for the luggage. The reader may remember that we had had one "reunion" at AT in October after she got back home from Macau (the ship "Adventurer" moving on to the South Pacific and eventually around the Cape of Magellan and on up the Atlantic to Lisbon), Amy then with some needed R and R before the next scheduled AT trip. I haven't mentioned that weekend in Los Angeles yet, suffice to say we got a warm greeting at AT from Susan Gillian. There was much talk about "Around Brazil" and what a success it had been; adventurer feedback had come in, all raving about the experience, Steve Barber Adventure Leader had sent his report, and they had a letter from Harry Downing the veteran of AT trips around the world as well.

The rest of that long weekend was different – Mike getting to know Amy off the ship, off work, and perhaps on all new turf. Okay, it's corny, but we decided to relive younger days and do Disneyland and throw in the Getty Museum for good measure. Both of us agreed California beaches were not up to Recife, Bahia and Rio, but we drove out to Pacific Palisades and watched the sea lions and birds down below. There were intimate moments at night back at the hotel, but the daytime tourism, holding hands, laughing a lot and just being together was terrific. On Sunday I flew back to Omaha, the commuter van to Lincoln and classes Monday morning. Amy would be back on "Adventurer" in the Mediterranean and then over to the Caribbean, Panama Canal and West Coast of

South America and the Galapagos. We left it with a promise for another rendezvous soon.

So you're filled in and now, five months later, I can tell of what turned out to be a great five days with Amy in Denver and Los Angeles, and the next phase of the plan for Pre-Columbian Meso America. In Denver Mr. and Mrs. Carrier welcomed me, and we had a drink out on the patio of their large home on a shady side street near to the big park in Denver with the Natural History Museum I remembered as a wide-eyed 10 year old on his first visit to a big city, a rare summer vacation for a Nebraska farmer and his family. Jack and Irene were hospitable, friendly and full of questions for me. Amy had talked of how we met, the trip to Brazil (and promised to get them a copy of "Around Brazil"), saying we were "just friends" but maybe a good match. Mrs. Carrier asked about the Gaherty name (Irish) and would that mean Catholic (yes) and said that matched the Carrier background (French and Catholic). I joked it would make me take up French again after a translation course in graduate school a few years ago. They both had been to France three or four times, loved Paris and had shown (dragged) Amy along once as a very young girl. "The Eiffel Tower was great, the cafés fun, but I really got tired at that ole' Louvre," Amy said, saying maybe AT could swing a few days for her and me to revisit soon.

We went down to the Brown Palace for dinner, I guess a "must" for Denver, and Amy and I got out to the Natural History Museum the next day where those dioramas had provided one of the great early thrills of a farm boy's life. We flew out of Stapleton late that afternoon with reservations at what else? a Marriott in Westwood not far from AT's office. We did tell her parents of the general plan for Mexico and Mesoamerica and our "partnership" in planning; Jack laughed and said "Have fun and be careful." Irene said the opposite, "Be careful and have fun." No questions asked or answered as to accommodations, but hey, neither of us were teenagers anymore. I think I mentioned Amy was 29 and me 31 on the ship last year.

We talked of the upcoming meeting during the flight, both agreeing there were a lot of nuts and bolts to be worked out the next three months. That was not that long a time to nail down itinerary and a lot more actual objectives and plans for the trip. The jet rolled into Los Angeles International amidst the smog, no bags were lost or delayed, and we were in a taxi to the Marriott just in time to hit rush hour in Los Angeles. For experienced trip planners this was a lousy start. After the two hours of stop and go we were just ready for a drink, dinner in the hotel, and getting some rest before the meeting with Susan and James tomorrow.

Up at seven, breakfast by eight, and a short taxi ride to the AT Headquarters on Wilshire, on the 6th floor of one of the shiny high rises all over Westwood. We saw Susan first; she and Amy were old friends, dealing with personnel on a couple of dozen AT trips. Susan gave me a big embrace and said, "So I get to meet 'Arretado' again, [the nickname Chico Buarque gave me in Brazil – "cool guy"] is that right?" And she laughed. I said, "It's Mike, Michael Gaherty and I want to thank you once again for taking a chance on me on 'Adventurer.'" She said, "A wise decision on all accounts, but let's meet James and say everything all at once, no need to repeat things and nothing left out." She picked up the phone, pushed what looked like a very well-worn button, spoke a minute or two and said, "Let's go down to the hall and meet the really important person here at AT."

James Morrison was a surprisingly young executive, perhaps just a bit on the other side of 45, tall, balding, with the "granny" glasses in vogue (we all liked John Denver, how could a nature expedition outfit not like a guy who sailed with Jacque Cousteau and wrote "Calypso" and "West Virginia" and "Rocky Mountain High?") He rose from his very cluttered desk, shook my hand and said, "Welcome Mike, you are now part of a very exclusive and may I say successful club." He nodded at Susan and gave Amy a big hug saying "My favorite Assistant Adventure Leader. Amy, I hope you aren't any the worse for wear and we haven't been working you too hard? I hear you and Mike helped each other 'ease the pain' in Brazil." Amy turned a bit red and me too. "Don't worry - nothing to get nervous about. Steve told me there was great chemistry all around on that trip."

I piped up, "A bit presumptuous of me but if you want the whole story it soon will be out, you know, a professor's ramblings: "Around Brazil on the 'International Adventurer.'" It might cut back on the gossip around the ship, or hey, maybe add to it." James smiled and said he would add it to the stack of "must reads."

"I've scheduled about an hour and a half for our meeting, but am hoping I can have you all for dinner at a famous old place in Los Angeles, 'Dave Chasen's.' You country folks from Colorado and Nebraska may have heard of it if you've read of the Hollywood Days. Susan is from Newport and knows every famous place in L.A. and she can give us the 'scoop' on the place. How about it?" Not ones to turn down such an invitation we both quickly agreed, and I blurted out I was a big W.C. Fields fan and had read of his many visits to Chasen's. Susan laughed and said, "Hey you're right and you probably know his friends never knew if he would either pick up the check and tip the waitress $100 or sit tight and see who else might pay! James is like him, just kidding! 6:00 p.m. I've already made the reservations, early for L. A. but it's a busy place later on in the evening."

"So, to work," James interjected. "We've got three issues to discuss, the Mesoamerica Pre – Columbian Research Trip the most important. I'd just like to address Mike briefly first on the future at AT and give him something to think about back in Lincoln. Maybe you two girls can wait just a few minutes in Susan's office and I'll buzz you to rejoin us? (The girls left and I was alone with James in the office.) "Mike, I'll just apprise you of my report from Steve Barber after the 'Around Brazil' trip and just as important Harry Downing's telephone talk with me just a month ago. You received top-notch reviews by the way. First of all, we'd like to have you on a reprise of 'Around Brazil' but probably not until 1976, but we would need a year's planning, starting in Spring 1975. I think the itinerary would be the same, 'Adventurer' is available and Captain Tony is amenable, and best of all it would work out during summer recess from your university. We would do a single contract with you for salary but at a substantial increase, and hopefully same staff. I think you should mull this over and give me a response sometime this fall in 1973. What's your reaction?"

"I'm honored and thrilled. I've already thought of the possibility and think foremost that the three-year hiatus between last summer and 1976 is a good idea. I might have a change or two in itinerary, but still with the same stops, maybe adding Santos and Curitiba and the Morretes Train. So I'll talk to you in September."

"Good. Now to more complicated stuff. Harry Downing told me he talked to you about possibly replacing him at AT for the Mexico, Central and South America trips and the one in Europe for Portugal and Spain. He is ready to scale back his work, but the good news is we would still have him as Adventure Leader for Europe for part of the year; he might even join you for the Spain-Portugal trip; he said you two were a good one-two 'punch' for the adventurers. The latter trip is coming up, scheduled for late Spring of 1977. Brochure deadline Spring of 1976. Is your head swimming yet? We have to keep a dozen balls in the air to keep this operation going. And are you confident of your expertise to do 'Cultural Speaker' for Spain and Portugal? I know you've got the 'book learning,' a Ph.D. in Spanish and Golden Age Literature (I've thoroughly studied your C.V.). But no 'in-country' experience except for study. Your reaction?"

"James, I can bone up on college notes, do more research and handle an overview of places, people and culture and love doing it. I would have to totally rely on local experts and guides for the actual on-shore excursions. This one is a tougher decision, but maybe with Harry along it could work out. I'd have to see it as 'post – grad' study, research and work. Oh yeah, there is the complication with classes during the Spring Term at U. of N. but I'm thinking a request for a leave of absence would not be turned down. Since that would come without pay, perhaps AT could take that into consideration. James smiled and said, "It's not the first rodeo for us along that line, as you Nebraskans say. It can be worked out." I added, perhaps they could work Amy's schedule to do the same trip. James smiled, thought for a moment, and said it was a distinct possibility. "It will depend what other trips are happening, our needs for personnel, and of course Amy's decision of what to do. I suspect I already know her preferences along that line."

"James, I'm wondering, re - thinking, you know, as much as I'd love to do it, the Spain − Portugal trip is every Spanish Ph.D.'s dream, like the Holy Grail I once said, maybe we should table Portugal − Spain for now. I'm thinking this Mexico- Mesoamerica venture is more important. And if all goes well in the research, we would do it, I mean, the finalized trip with Adventurers, in summer of next year in 1975."

"I guess Mike that what I'm trying to do is be sure you will be available and we can have your services. We do not see this as a short − term relationship; we are looking to the future. Like I say, without the incredible recommendations I've got from all concerned it wouldn't happen, and we at AT are taking a bit of a chance. There's some time to think and my phone line is always open. We'll talk some more later. Let's call the ladies and think of Mexico and Pre-Columbian now.

With everyone back in the room I guess you could say we "brainstormed" for Mexico and other options. There were lots of questions: What precisely are the goals of the finalized trip for AT adventurers? Travel? What is the intellectual objective of what it is to be seen and experienced and learned? Level of travel and lodging accommodations − are they up to AT's standards? What AT staff would be on the trip? Local guides and expertise? Cost? Is Mexico enough? Is it too much to include Guatemala (Tikal and Quiriguá) and Copán? Could they be post − trip excursions or a separate trip? Obviously, we would need a tentative itinerary before deciding that. I had brought along my original plan, giving a copy to James, saying Amy already had a copy as well as James Hansen in New York. And not the least important would be a title for the trip (s).

I. Mexico - The Tentative Itinerary

Day 1.	Settling in at the Hotel María Isabel
Day 2.	Preamble to the Trip: The National Museum of History and Anthropology - Mexico City
Day 3.	Teotihuacán, Tula
Days 4, 5	Mexico City
	(Tenochtitlán)
	El Zócalo, El Templo Mayor, la Catedral
	Diego Rivera Mural: "Historia de México," Palacio Nacional, Bellas Artes
	La Villa de Guadalupe, la Virgen de Guadalupe
	La Casa Azul: Frida Kahlo and Diego Rivera
	The National University and Mosaic Library
Day 6.	Flight to Oaxaca and Hotel and Dinner
	El Hotel Camino Real
Day 7, 8.	La Plaza Central
	La Casa de Hernán Cortés
	La Iglesia de Santo Domingo
	La Iglesia de los Jesuitas
	El Mercado Indio
	Local Museums? Rufino Tamayo Museum?
Day 9.	Bus or Vans to Monte Albán, Mitla
Day 10.	Flight to Tuxla Gutiérrez, bus to San Cristóbal de las Casas, Chiapas. Hotel Diego Mazariegos
Day 11.	In San Cristóbal
	El Mercado Indio
	Maya Weaving Cooperative
	La Casa de Nho Nablom
Day 12.	San Juan Chamula, free time San Cristóbal
Day 13.	Bus/ Vans to Palenque

	Agua azul,
	Palenque – Hotel Misol Ha?
Days 14, 15.	Palenque the Archeological Site
Day 16.	Bus to Villa Hermosa
	The Olmecs, Las Ventas Museum
	Late p.m. flight to Mérida in the Yucatán
	Hotel Holiday Inn
Day 17.	In Mérida
	Casa de Montejo
	La Plaza
	Old Museum
	Modern Fountain
Day 19.	Maya Link to Mexico and Guatemala: Uxmal
Day 20.	Toltec – Maya Link to Mexico: Chichén – Itzá
	Possible Post Trip Extension: R and R: the Riviera Maya?
	Cancún
	Tulúm

II. Pre – Columbian Heritage: Guatemala and Honduras

Day 1.	Flight to Guatemala City – Hotel
Day 2.	Kaminaljuyu – Olmec- Maya – Teotihuacano
	National Palace
	Archeological Museum
Day 3.	Vans to Antigua Hotel?
	Antigua: Ciudad Vieja, Antigua - Plaza, Conventos, Shopping
Day 4.	San Antonio Aguas Calientes. Town and weaving, Iglesia de San Francisco, Iglesia de Santo Domingo
Day 5.	Vans to Lago de Atitlán, Barco to Santiago Atitlán
Day 6.	Hikes around Lake, fishing, free time, Casa Contenta Dinner

Day 7.   Mercado de Chichicastenango, Hotel?
Day 8.   Bus to Guatemala City, Flight to Flores
Day 9, 10.   Tikal, Archeological Site, Museum, Hike in Forest.
                Exploration. Hotel?
Day 10.   Excursion to Quiriguá
Day 11.   Return to Guatemala City
Day 12.   Van to town of Copán, Honduras
Day 13.   Copán Ruínas
Day 14.   Return to Guatemala City. Flight Home

There was an immediate reaction to the outline by all; unless the outline were drastically modified, it would have to be two separate trips. James wanted to know the rationale for each trip, in effect, the objective and how it would fit into AT's expedition tradition. The trick is to match the objective perfectly with the trip title. It might seem easy but it is not. If the aim is to provide an overview of Pre – Columbian Civilization in Mexico (or Guatemala), the archeological sites are the main focus. But if one is adding in the major cities near the sites, that is another matter. Meaning: a change in title. I suggested "An Overview of Pre – Columbian Civilization in Mexico plus Its Gateway Cities." That way, the travel experience, transportation and lodging and tourism would be on perhaps equal footing, and Amy would provide the expertise to make that a great AT experience. I assured James that the all-important flow of time and sequencing of the development of civilization in the area was on sound footing with the itinerary.

"You can trust me on the accuracy of all this. I've done the research, endlessly checked reliable sources in graduate school, and have hands on experience at the sites. Let me put it this way, if I were a curious, enthusiastic traveler and veteran of AT trips, I would salivate at the possibilities."

James said, "Mr. Gaherty you are putting yourself out on a limb on this. We can't make mistakes. You are aware the whole thinking is for AT to do something new with land travel; it's got to be good and it's got to be enticing."

"James, if it means anything, I think the NYT's James Hansen's interest and endorsement might make all of us feel a little more relaxed and confident. In all humility he knows what I can do, have done in the past and believes in me. (I felt like I was applying to graduate school all over again.)"

"Okay there are four of us here. What do the rest of you think?"

Amy said, "I'm all in; I've already begun checking and there are some downright fabulous cities, towns, accommodations and travel experiences to be had."

Susan said, "I'm confident we already have AT personnel, naturalists, and James Hansen can add top flight National Geographic photographers. This is an opportunity for AT and certainly worth the investment of Mike and Amy's research trip. One factor to be worked out, all important, is a network of local guides, and local transportation. That puts a large burden on Amy. Are you up to it?"

"My last four years at Marriott and AT have been doing precisely that. Yes, you can count on it."

James Morrison smiled and closed the meeting, "Fine. Full speed ahead. I'll expect a detailed and final report in September. You will have the use of AT credit cards, or travelers' checks or cash plus trip insurance. I suspect you will need all of them. I'll expect interim reports. It's pretty exciting; there are already many options for the entire area, but maybe you can make AT – NYT Travel the best. When will you start?"

"I looked at Amy and said U of N classes and exams will be over June 1; I could travel on June 15 and I anticipate no more than six weeks to do the entire thing. If you can spare Amy for June and July, I'll return her to you in good shape, taking into account R and R from our trip and working out the final report and plan, all by let's say September 1. And I'll be back in the classroom shortly thereafter."

All agreed and James said he would see us all at Chasen's at 6:00 p.m. It was not what I imagined; comfortable chairs at tables, large leather covered booths, but not a "fine dining" look (but it did have the prices). What makes the place is that it is plastered with large photos of Hollywood Stars, more old than new. Clark Gable, Gary Cooper, John Wayne, Mae West, Hedy Lamar, Doris Day, Liz Taylor, Eva Gardner and more. The comedians were represented, George Burns and Gracie Allen, Lucille Ball and Desi Arnaz, the Marx Brothers and of course W.C. Fields. I got a chance to ramble on about all the Fields' movies, but Susan was really in charge, a true "expert" on Hollywood History. Great fun. Good food, James choose the wine, and we all talked of the trip to come and toasted our good fortune. The latter turned out to be much needed.

3

———◆◆◆———

FLYING DOWN TO MEXICO

The venture started out as planned; I flew into Denver from Omaha on June 14th, met Amy at her folks' house and had a nice dinner, and we checked documents, clothes, writing supplies and a small tape recorder and flew out of Stapleton on Mexicana mid-morning on the 15th. The flight was three and one-half hours so we had a chance to go over the outline of the plan, the itinerary and the objectives in Mexico City. We were both excited to be going on what we anticipated would be much more than work, but rather a great adventure.

No matter how much study or practice in Spanish one has, it is still a shock to fly into that huge, smoggy airport at 7000 feet in the Valley of Mexico, arrive in what they call "México D.F." [Mexico City, Federal District, like our D.C.] and be greeted by nothing but Spanish all around you. Amy and I were both about on an even par in facility in Spanish, me more book learning and reading of literature, she more in the day to day living. That was a good thing as it turned out. AT did have an agent in Mexico City, Roberto Maya with a small office on busy Avenida Insurgentes, and he would be our liaison the next few days. Traffic was heavy, but our taxi maneuvered in and out of the many lanes of the new freeway to the city, dodging what seemed like totally uncontrolled cars, many of them the ubiquitous yellow taxis in D.F. (but not the red "peseros" from my student days on El Paseo de la Reforma), trucks and buses belching exhaust fumes, and dozens and dozens of motorcycles. We arrived to a familiar scene to me, the famous Paseo de la Reforma, the most beautiful boulevard in Mexico City, designed, if you can believe local folklore, by Emperor Maximillian in the 19th century at the command of wife Carlota, a thoroughfare guiding him straight home from work in the Zócalo to the Palace in Chapultepec Park! I surmise there were some delays and excuses.

The Hotel María Isabel was number one on Amy's checklist for AT adventurers in Mexico City; there were lots of reasons. It was built in 1962 by Patiño the Bolivian Tin King (think of the famous Potosi gold and silver mine of colonial days). This was incidentally about the same time as the "Torre Latinoamericana," Mexico's first and foremost skyscraper, forty stories high in the land of earthquakes and rare air. For me the hotel had a special memory. I was studying at the National University of Mexico the year it opened in 1962, and in that amazing pre-boom economy, we buddy students from the UNAM actually went to the roof bar, listened to a soft Jazz Trio, and drank Dos Equis beers for one dollar each. We even took dates and sat on the outdoor roof patio, listened to music and danced a bit. The beer or two took up the evening budget (we had taken our dates to dinner earlier in a modest bullfight themes place just across Reforma), but what a thrill. A glass skyscraper in Mexico City!

But there were other reasons to be there – a great location, one of the best in Mexico City now eleven years later. The setting was a bit breathtaking – near the Glorieta and the tall column with the "Ángel de la Independencia" in gold paint, commemorating Mexico's moment of Independence from Spain in 1810, done in the notorious regime of Porfirio Díaz in 1910. Down Reforma to the northeast was the historic center with the Zócalo, Plaza Mayor, Government Palace and the National Cathedral. The other direction was Mexico City's main "green spot," the Forest of Chapultepec with the old Military Academy and Zoo, a huge park and to one side the most exclusive living in the city, "Lomas de Chapultepec."

Amy and I concluded that even though Mexico City was in a huge building phase in 1973 and new construction (partially to get ready for the Olympics in 1974), including hotels everywhere, the María Isabel had to be Adventurers' "Home Away from Home." Check that off! After a drink at the outside bar overlooking Reforma, I convinced Amy to do a bit of "nostalgia" with me, dinner at a tourist "must," Sanborn's of Mexico in the Zona Rosa just a few blocks' walk (if you can manage to cross Reforma way down at a traffic light). Hotel staff said to not carry documents and too much cash, it was a notorious area for the "rateros" or Mexico City pickpockets. Good advice. In my time in 1962 Sanborn's with its beautiful tiled interior was <u>the</u> place for middle- and upper-class Mexicans to take their family for café, snacks and small meals, and for the tourists. I celebrated with a Club Sandwich "torta" and a bottle of Dos Equis beer, Amy with the "plato mexicano" of taco, enchilada, arroz y frijol, her stomach much better than mine. Have I mentioned my travel necessity yet in this book? i.e. Pepto Bismol tablets and a lot of them!

Back to the hotel and our twin beds in a "business suite" overlooking Reforma, we mapped out the next three days. We had agreed to replicate the agenda for the proposed "Adventurer" trip. We would begin at Roberto Maya's office the next morning with his orientation and supplying a van and driver for the itinerary. A taxi to his office on Insurgentes and away we would go. We had a couple of drinks, both of us agreeing that this city was overwhelming and we had not scratched the surface. We also agreed to start the adventure with saying hello again in some intimate time, a good way to begin the next four weeks.

I'm hesitant to tell it but there was one dark moment. At breakfast the next morning, a gentleman in a dark business suit approached our table, introduced himself as Jaime Torres and politely asked for a moment of our time. We had no reason to not oblige after all we were in a sense "guests" in Mexico. He said (all in Spanish) that he was an agent of Mexico's national intelligence force, the "Policía Federal," that the agency was aware of our "mission" in Mexico and that it was approved by them, but that there was one slightly disturbing bit of information he wanted to pass on to us.

A small but important organization called the "Defensa del Patrimonio Nacional" or DPN according to Jaime; a splinter group "living in the past" and promoting "Mexico for the Mexicans" has been recently opposing national efforts to increase tourism, including the vast development by the López Portillo regime of the "New Acapulco" on the Caribbean Coast. They have a small number of representatives in the national congress, rarely making waves, but a thorn in the side of the progressive modern Mexico. Word has come to the PF of their opposition to any major efforts of "watering down" the Indigenous Heritage for the consumption of "ignorant tourists invading the country." Jaime said it all is indeed absurd, totally out of sync with the times, but sporadically sponsored crimes and violence against tourists and tour companies have taken place. The government, naturally, has been keeping this quiet, investigating perpetrators and dealing with them, but that sporadic incidents, very isolated, have taken place.

Amy gasped, and I was in shock. "Why are you telling us this? Are we in danger? We are prepared to halt our project if we and future tours are to be targets of any kind of violence."

"Not at all, or rather, almost not at all. However, I am here to inform you that throughout your travels in Mexico, and we believe yours is a truly magnificent project, you will be under our protection and we will have agents, incognito of course, accompanying you at a distance to assure your success. For any reason that you may need to be in touch with us I am giving you my personal telephone number, available 24/7, in case of any problems. 05-033-3333. I have been specifically assigned by the National Director of Tourism in liaison with the PF to assist you. We simply believed and believe now that it is better for you to have this information and, as it were, an 'insurance policy' so you can do your work in a relaxed way and enjoy Mexico. You are aware that our country is not perfect and we simply want to ensure that our vision of opening Mexico and our heritage safely to the world is our priority."

I said, "Why haven't we heard or even had a whiff of this problem up to now? I know there are occasional robberies or muggings of tourists, but that's all over the world and Mexico is no exception."

"Mr. Gaherty and Miss Carrier, that is because we downplay any possible problems, after all, who then would come to Mexico? Consider this no more than the usual diplomatic appeal between our two countries for cooperation and progress. Please continue with your work; Roberto Maya I am sure will quell your concerns; he has worked with us for years and knows the ropes. You are in good hands."

The next morning we arrived at Roberto Maya's office, were welcomed with a steaming hot and sweet Mexican "cafecito" and had a brief conversation before joining our van driver Alberto for the first part of the research, the National Museum of Anthropology and History in Chapultepec Park which would provide an overview for us (and for future adventurers) of Pre − Columbian Mexico. Roberto was a long-time veteran of AT and had arranged the port stops for AT's previous ocean expeditions via Vera Cruz on the Atlantic and Acapulco on the Pacific. He remembered Amy from the "Adventurer" and said it was a pleasure to meet her in person. We explained our itinerary and he waxed enthusiastic saying it sounded terrific. Then I asked him about the visit from Jaime Torres of the PF. Roberto smiled and said, "No se preocupen! This is just standard procedure by the PF and I want to reassure you it's a good idea. By the way, the Mexican National Congress is full of such minority factions, not like your two − party system, and all have the right to express themselves. You are in no danger and in fact it will facilitate and iron out any 'wrinkles' should they come up. I'm in touch with Jaime and you have my phone number as well. I just wish I could go with you, I'm excited for AT and this new venture." After another good "cafecito" Roberto introduced us to Alberto "a veteran for our day to day in Mexico" and we were off through the traffic to Chapultepec.

We agreed to meet Alberto after the museum, at 4 p.m. He said he would be there to pick us up and take us back to the María Isabel. Tomorrow would be the Zócalo with the Cathedral, the Diego Rivera murals, the excavation of the Plaza Mayor, and finally the Museo de Bellas Artes in the a.m. and the University, the Villa de Guadalupe and Frida Kahlo in the p.m. Wow! We were both thinking that these would have to comprise at least two days of the adventurers' itinerary. We'll see.

We passed through Chapúltepec Forest and the high end residential section called "Las Lomas." Old timers will recall that in the days of the 1950s and 1960s when one read Carlos Fuentes' "Where the Air is Clear" ("La Región Más Transparente del Aire") or "The Death of Artemio Cruz ("La Muerte de Artemio Cruz"), classics of Mexican Literature, "Las Lomas" was THE place to live for upper class Mexicans. In 1973 it seemed not quite so impressive, but what was truly impressive was our stop at …

4

---◆◆◆---

THE GREAT "MUSEO NACIONAL DE ANTROPOLOGÍA E HISTORIA"

This would be Amy's and my own first big event on the trip itinerary, but the visits to the actual Pre-Colombian sites later would provide the large part of the research for the trip for adventurers. I've included the photos because they will be part of the report and essential should AT and NYTT approve of what we saw. The museum offers both an introduction to and a panoramic view of Pre-Columbian Mexico. The huge umbrella-like bronze entrance to the museum with low-relief sculpture to both sides, Pre-Columbian to one, Western culture to the other, is indeed impressive. And the front entrance sports the same symbol as on the Mexican national flag, the eagle on the cactus with a snake in its mouth (from the Aztec myth of seeing the eagle and thus knowing to settle at that spot, in this case the Valley of Mexico and build their capital city of Tenochtitlán). The museum was opened in 1964, just two years after my initial study in Mexico at the UNAM, during the presidency of Adolfo López Mateos at a cost of $20 million U.S.

As we take a deep breath and hope for the energy to see it all, an overview of Pre-Columbian Mexico lies before us. Successive rooms or "salones" show the major cultures and civilizations, no small task. These notes and accompanying photos are in no sense a "history" of the diverse cultures, but simply the highlights from this outstanding museum, the best of its kind in the world. They will provide the basis for AT's and NYTT's plan. My understanding of Pre − Columbian Culture comes in part from hours of study of books on this place. Amy like me had not seen it either, but we were "agog" with all that came before our eyes the next few hours. Each culture will be seen in detail and we will travel later to many of these archeological sites in our "gira" [tour] of Mexico.

THE TEOTIHUACÁN ROOM

150 BC to 650 A.D. "The Place Where the Men Became Gods" – this was the Aztec saying created centuries later when speaking of Teotihuacán. The place was a commercial, architectural and religious center which dominated Mesoamerica from the Valley of México to the Maya area to the south. It was noted for its ceramics, sculpture, obsidian, "fresco" paintings, large pyramids and the first example of the cult of Quetzalcóatl, the Plumed Serpent. Along with the Olmecs and the pre-classic Mayas, it was one of the "proto – culturas" of Mexico.

In the Teotihuacán room is a reproduction of the Temple of Quetzalcóatl the Plumed Serpent in its supposed original colors. There is a view of the "Ciudadela," the long avenue of the center of Teotihuacán. The temple walls were originally of stucco, painted in vivid colors. The Pryamid of the Sun is on one end facing East, the Pryamid of the Moon on the other facing west.

Temple of Quetzalcóatl

On one wall of the salon is a scene of the environs of Teotihuacán, a mural by Nicolás Moreno, and the great monolith (single stone) of the goddess "Chalchiutlicue," the "Great Goddess of Teotihuacán," a goddess of water. This huge stone was found in the plaza in front of the pyramid of the moon. One scholar says that the hands seem to be wringing water from the "huipil" or blouse, "as if freeing the power of the mountain called 'Cerro Gordo' (behind the pyramid of the moon) for her people." There is indeed much speculation as to the exact name of this god.

One sees an excellent example of a mask from Teotihuacán with turquoise, serpentine, onyx and pieces of shell, one of the prizes of the museum. The masks represent anonymous faces, neither masculine nor feminine, neither young nor old. They were placed on the deceased to give "good appearance" to the dead person for their arrival in "the other world." This was done throughout Mesoamerica, and some of the best masks are in Europe because of European excavation of the sites and/or dealings between Spain and the countries of America after Independence. The salon also has a reproduction of one of the "frescos," paintings on plaster, of Teotihuacán, from the "tablero" or vertical wall of a temple.

THE TULA ROOM

Atlante from Tula

Tula, near Teotihuacán, is another name for "Tollán," the place of the reeds. This room has the huge images of the "Atlantes," probably warrior-soldiers ready for battle with an "atlatl" or throwing spear in their hand and a breastplate with the image of the butterfly (symbol of the war god) and a headdress looking like a drum. The statues of the "Atlantes" were used to support the wooden beams of the temple of Tlahuizcal-Pantecujtli in Tula. They are four to six meters in height.

The guidebook of the museum says that Tula was founded by the people called Chichimecas who arrived in the area during the time of the decline of Teotihuacán and who lived side by side with the Teotihuacán people and adopted much of their culture. The city or center of Tula was abandoned around 1150 A.D. and its people whom we know as Toltecs migrated in two directions. One group moved to the Valley of Mexico where they established themselves and became the dominant group around Lake Texcoco; the other moved to the east and south and eventually to the Yucatán. At Chichén-Itzá they formed a hybrid civilization with late post-classic Mayas (the Itzáes). It was the Toltecs who took the cult of Quetzalcóatl to the Yucatán where the god became known as Kukulcán in Maya, "The Feathered Serpent."

An entirely different version of the theory: the Toltec people originated near Cuernavaca and their first leader-chief was Mixcóatl; his son in turn was the man Quetzalcóatl. In this salon there is a beautiful mural showing the supposed manner of construction of a pyramid at Tula, the workers pulling/pushing the upper part of a statue of an "Atlante" to the summit.

Chacmool

In the same room there is a carved stone representation of what we call the "Chacmool" found in front of a palace or temple of Tula. It represents the reclined figure of a warrior, and these were placed in front of the temples. The "platillo" or plate on the chest was used for sacrificial offerings. Another representation of the "chacmooles" is that they are water gods. Mexican writer Carlos Fuentes' famous short story, "Chacmool," has a marvelous twist on the theme. They are also seen in Chichén – Itzá, the Toltec – Late Maya city in the Yucatán.

THE "MEXICA" ROOM

The "Mexica" are of course the same as the Aztecs; the name comes from "Mixcóatl" one of the early leaders as per the legend. And of course all this gave rise to the name of the country, "Mexico." Their city was founded by the wandering Aztecs, when according to legend, they spied a tall cactus with an eagle on top with a snake in its mouth. Thus: the city became Tenochtitlán in the midst of a great lake, Texcoco.

In a central part of the room is the architectural plan of the city of Tenochtitlán, the original Aztec capital.

Aztec Calendar, Sun God

Next is the famous round stone carving of the Sun God or "The Aztec Calendar." This is the most famous monument of Aztec Mexico. It actually was a sculpture dedicated to the sun and not a calendar. It weighs 24.5 tons and is 3.57 meters tall. It was made in 1479 during the reign of Axayacatl, the sixth emperor of the Aztecs, and was placed in front of the Great Temple ("El Templo Mayor") of Tenochtitlán. With the conquest and destruction of the city by the Spaniards in 1521, the Spaniards ordered the stone to be buried in the main plaza, "La Plaza Mayor." It was only rediscovered in 1790 and moved to a site near the Metropolitan Cathedral; in 1885 it was moved again to the old Anthropology Museum. There are twenty "glyphs" or symbols of the day and an "earth monster" in the center, perhaps representing the sun fallen to earth. There is a diadem around the monster. The stone indicates the four prior ages to the present one in 1479, that is, the four previous suns, and it shows cataclysms, not dates. (All this is according to the experts of the museum.)

Coatlicue, Mother of the Gods

This is a statue or carved image of the famous or infamous Coatlicue, "She of the Skirt of Serpents." The image was accidentally discovered in 1790 and reburied several times by the authorities. She is the "earth mother," the mother of Huitzilopochtli (the sun) and Coyolxauqui, (the moon). Coatlicue is seen with her head cut off, two serpents in its place and symbols of flowing blood. Her hands and feet are in the form of the "talons" of a bird, and she sports a necklace of hands and hearts. Amy and I both agreed that it possibly may make your blood curl!

An aside is to be permitted. This image alone, but principally, sent shudders up my spine and reflects I believe the absolute terror that much of the Aztec culture can instill. The Sun Monster comes in a close second. The darkness and the somberness of the Aztec sculptures are a huge contrast to the realism and beauty of Maya art and sculpture, a reflection I think of the two world views.

There is a famous legend: Coyolxauqui the goddess of the moon and the stars plots to kill her mother, Coatlicue, but her son Huitzilopochtli the Sun god comes to the rescue and defeats his sister and the stars. There was an incredible archeological find during the construction of the subway in Mexico City just before Amy and I arrived in the early 1970s; they unearthed a large, round stone depicting pieces of a woman. The stone, perhaps, symbolizes the victory of the day (the sun) over the evil forces of the night (the moon, the stars) and the necessity of daily sacrifice of sacred blood (called "Chauchihuatl") to sustain the sun on his daily journey of conquering the night. It is the basis, according to some scholars, of the concept of Aztec sacrifice!

The Stone of Tizoc

The stone shows the Aztec Emperor, but dressed in the clothing of Tezcatlipoca, god of the smoking mirror, a figure repeated fifteen times in the stone. Tezcatlipoca harks back to Toltec culture and the legend of the battle between the forces of evil represented by Tezcatlipoca and the forces of good, represented by Quetzalcóatl. Tezcatlipoca tricked Quetzalcóatl, got him drunk and told him he had sexual relations with his own sister. Quetzalcóatl was so ashamed he left Tula and migrated to the East to the Yucatán. Note that this is just <u>one </u>of the many legends of Quetzalcóatl.

The Temple Stone or "Teocalli" was found near Moctezuma's palace in 1831. It is believed to be his actual throne. It carries the date of 1507 and depicts the fire ceremony which took place each 52 years. Above the seat of the throne is a representation of the "Earth Monster" ("Monstruo de la Tierra") with the sun disk at his back (thus "supporting the sun"). Therefore, Moctezuma gave the impression of actually carrying the sun itself on his back. Looking at the same Teocalli stone from the rear one sees two seated deities, drawing blood from their own bodies, from the genitals. The blood served as penitence and sustenance for the kingdom.

Another aside: it is interesting to note the Spanish and Catholic concept of a god who sacrificed himself, his own body and blood, for mankind's redemption. This was a concept not strange to the Aztecs. The Spaniards employed a rather ingenious use of the belief while "evangelizing" the conquered tribes.

THE OAXACA ROOM: ZAPOTEC AND LATER MIXTEC CULTURES

There is a replica of a "fresco" from Tomb 105 at Monte Albán. The "fresco" shows nine pairs (husband and wife) in a procession with glyphs that name the people, representing the ancestors who welcome the deceased person in the tomb to "the next life." Some of the headdresses have traits of the Teotihuacán style, thus indicating their time, 150-650 A.D. Monte Albán was contemporary to Teotihuacán and later Tula.

The Famous "Danzantes" or "Dancers" of Monte Albán

Danzante from Monte Alban

There were originally some 140 figures. They are done in "low relief" and are said to depict men with their eyes closed, supposedly dead, all naked. In the genital area of some there is a "text" with supposed genital mutilation. It is thought that all represent victims of war, and that this in its totality is a monument or memorial to the victors and their victims.

THE MAYA ROOM

The Mayas are along with the Olmecs and Teotihuacán one of the proto – cultures of Mexico. Dating from pre – classic times well before Christ to the Classic Period ending in about 900 A.D., they prove to have a world view, religious and artistic concepts very different from Central Mexico. After the still unproven collapse of the Classical Era, remnants of that civilization migrated to the Yucatán and eventually founded another great civilization, the hybrid Toltec – Maya.

Tomb of Pacal at Palenque

With at least a dozen major archeological sites in Mexico, Palenque in Chiapas State was just one of them, but perhaps the most beautiful due to its buildings, sculptures, "frescos" and its location in the middle of the rich, wet jungle of Chiapas State. Pacal was a major king at Palenque. His tomb was discovered in 1952 by Mexican archeologist, Alberto Rus. The king's sarcophagus is seen with bones, jade and cinnabar ornaments. The sculpted stone covering the tomb is a famous Maya sculpture: it is said to represent King Pacal at the moment of death, falling into the jaws of the Earth Monster (Death), into the "underworld" or "infraworld" as if he "were being swallowed by the jaws of the skeleton of the underworld." To the side of the sarcophagus are the images of ten figures, believed to be either relatives or counselors. The temple is unique in Mesoamerica: a pyramid and temple built <u>before</u> the death of a king and probably according to his own design.

Next in the Maya Room is a "Dintel" or "Lintel" n. 43 from Yaxchilán, a Classic Period site on the frontier between Mexico and Guatemala near Bonampak, yet another site unique for its "frescos." A king of the jaguar lineage has a symbol of power in his hand. Facing him is a woman also of royal linage, dressed in a "huipil" [blouse] which has designs still used today in the region! She offers him a rope with spines indicating self-bloodletting.

Reproduction of One of the Frescos of Bonampak (Classic Maya)

Bonampak was a small, "minor" classic Maya site, ahá! Except for one thing: it contains the remains of the most complete, fascinating, and colorful of the Maya wall paintings called "frescos" (I mentioned that no less than Diego Rivera was influenced by them in doing his "Historia de México" to come). This reproduction stands out in the Museum.

Maya Mural, Bonampak

Beneath a king (to the left) who dances are two "priests" who subject a naked man with the bowed body, hands and feet tied, a captive it is surmised. Above them are, perhaps, the "executioner" armed with a knife who prepares to open the chest of the victim to take out his heart and offer it to the supernatural powers. A question immediately arises: is this proof of human sacrifice among the previously thought "philosopher kings" of the Mayas or just another act of war?

GULF COAST ROOM

The Olmecs located on the southeast coast of Mexico on the Tehuántepec Peninsula are still shrouded in mystery, but current belief is that they are the earliest of major Pre – Columbian Cultures in Mexico and either share with or passed to the ancient Maya much of their culture. Hundreds of years before Christ. It is surmised the beginning of Maya hieroglyphic writing and the basis for the Long Count of Mathematics may have originated with the Olmecs. But they left only what one may consider the "beginnings" of centers, construction of temples that the Classic Maya would perfect. The huge carved heads are the most famous artefact.

Olmec Carved Head

A huge presence in the salon is one of the giant sculpted heads from the Olmec culture (San Lorenzo, Tres Zapotes or la Venta).

4:00 p.m. arrived and we were as surmised totally exhausted, but both in total agreement that the first stop or activity of the trip should be the Museum. Hopefully it would not scare travelers off, thinking "this is too much for me." Rather, it would prepare all of us for an exciting twenty days in Mexico. Alberto drove us to the Hotel and after drinks in the room and about two hours of talk and note -taking and comparison of the day's experience I talked Amy into dinner and entertainment at my favorite place from student days in Mexico – the Spanish motif restaurant Las Gitanerías [The Gypsies] with food, wine, and an after dinner show of excellent, legitimate Spanish "flamenco" with dancers, "cantaores" and guitarists.

One guitarist in particular, David Moreno, now well into near retirement age but no less a performer, was still there, a memory of student days. We got a chance to talk to him during the break. I introduced Amy and spoke of our project and timidly but hopefully asked if he would be available for a short classic performance for our adventurers the following year. "Si quisiera Dios, siempre un placer, Miguel y Amy. Contanto que los dedos y la memoria no me fallen" (and he laughed). Understood of course there would be a nice gratuity from AT and NYTT. I guess I had jumped the gun before talking it all over with Amy but once again she was thrilled with the place, the terrific food, wine, ambiance and happy to put it on her list.

We were exhausted back at the hotel and after outlining the next day's activities both fell into deep sleep. We decided we would not need Alberto in the a.m. but for old times' sake would take a "pesero" on the Paseo de la Reforma and see the immensity of what the Plaza Mayor and Bellas Artes would offer. Alberto would pick us up in the p.m. and drive us to the south part of the city to see the mosaics of the National University Library and then to the Diego Rivera and Frida Kahlo Museum.

5

LA PLAZA MAYOR, MEXICO D.F.

We both awoke rested and after an "Americanized" breakfast of scrambled eggs, bacon and toast, but with those great "bolillos" with real butter and strawberry jam, and wonderful "café con leche," we packed water bottles, snacks and cameras along with note pads, pens and a good map of Mexico City and headed for the "Paseo de la Reforma." (Oh, as mentioned, for those of you who have read my books, in addition there was a good supply of Pepto Bismol. The "Latin Americanist" has a fragile gringo stomach.) The old "peseros" from my student days were still there (and along Avenida Insurgentes as well). The Mexican peso was still 12 to the dollar.

I can't help it. "I don't care if it rains or freezes as long as I've got my Plastic Jesus, on the dashboard of my car." Except, the "peseros" have all sizes of plastic statues of Our Lady of Guadalupe, pendants, banners and ribbons of saints, Popes, yes and even Jesus. Does this keep them safe? Perhaps. But not from wear and tear; like in 1962, many cars had at least one door wired shut (the farmer boy thinks baling wire) and often you could not use the shotgun seat. And the price was up – inflation and Mexico's booming economy – now a whopping 5 pesos (60 cents USD). This is capitalism at its best in a quasi-socialist – capitalist country. The drivers own their cars. Everybody for himself in a no holds barred business. The cars looked like refugees from Havana – Chevys, Fords, Plymouths – all

La Plaza Mayor, Mexico D.F. | 5

bright red (a **D.F.** rule), all shiny, in fact spotless, but when you got in and heard the missing motor and experienced the lurching starts and squeaking stops of the brakes, you believed it when the "choferes" proudly said they had 500,000 kilometers on them (the odometer long had stopped working). We flagged one down, jumped in the back seat with two other customers, Mexicans they were, and dodged traffic to the Zócalo. Amy said AT could afford regular taxis. "I've had the experience. Enough already!"

You think I'm kidding. The imminent Carlos Fuentes wrote his best-selling novel on Mexico City of 1958 with the main narrator one of these renegade taxi drivers. Seat belts had just started to come in back home, but no evidence of them here. We arrived safely in that huge national meeting place of Mexico, the "Plaza Mayor" in Aztec times and the "Zócalo" or city center with the Spaniards. The first thing you see is the huge Mexican flag flying in its center, the drab National Government Palace to one side, the huge Metropolitan Cathedral to its right, and old commercial and government buildings opposite. Amy and I were in awe even though I had seen it before, and just stood there trying to take it in. That is, stood to the side of the whirring traffic. We decided first stop should be the "Palacio de Gobierno."

Tourists are allowed to enter, noting there are armed guards with sub-machine guns to either side. The National Palace was intentionally built on the ruins of Moctezuma's original palace. The high point of the palace is discovered in an immense interior patio with a stairway to one side and the walls around it which house the great work of "frescos," the murals of Diego Rivera, his "History of Mexico." I'm including a highly detailed description of the murals in this report (to become the first "Letter" to James Hansen of the New York Times) first of all because they are an outstanding cultural artifact of modern Mexico, but secondly, because they tie in the political and philosophical concepts of the Revolution of 1910 and Pre-Columbian culture. Both are motives for our "field work" to come. AT and NYTT will use highlights of this information, we hope, for the travel brochures.

The National Palace has been the center of the Mexican National Government since 1821; it is located on the site of the Aztec Palace of Moctezuma which was later converted into the palace of the Conquistador Hernán Cortés, and then the palace of the viceroys of "Nueva España."

The "frescos" were commissioned or "encomendados" in 1929 to be done by Diego Rivera, and the result is his "History of Mexico." The "frescos" trace Mexican history from the fall of Teotihuacán around 650 A.D. to 1929. They comprise a "painted epic" with the main theme being the Mexican Revolution of 1910-1917, and the style is an "ultra- realism" to avoid "mal entendidos" or any possible mistakes in interpretation. The painter used the dialectic from Marxist theory, contrasting the evils of Spain, Mexican dictators of the national period and then foreign capitalists versus the goodness of the pre-conquest natives and the peasants of Mexico in the 20th century. His goal was to depict a modern workers' state. It should be noted in passing that the two main artistic influences on Rivera were the "frescos" of the Italian Renaissance, but just as importantly, the "frescos" of Pre-Colombian sites at Teotihuacán and Bonampak in southeastern Mexico.

The immense work took six total years to complete, the date of completion being 1951. Rivera himself said of it, (paraphrasing): "It is not a painting but a world in a mural." It is, in the final analysis, an allegoric or symbolic portrait of Mexico.

THE MURALS, AN INTRODUCTION

The Main Mural Diego Rivera

In the main mural, including the stairways, there are three large panels:

1. The Center: From the Conquest to the Revolution of 1910
2. The Right Stairway: Pre-Colombian Mexico without regard to the Emperor or a value judgment of the pre-conquest peoples
3. The Left Stairway: Modern Mexico

All have a "social, utopic vision."

The Central Panel of the Main Mural: General Description

There are five panels within the large panel dealing with the positive and negative aspects of Mexico via a Marxist Dialectic View (common in those days): history is either heroic or a history of treason and oppression. It is totally positive or negative, and there is no other way to see it according to Diego Rivera. The ideological premise for this panel is the national revolutionary history of Mexico from its origins in the Spanish conquest. Mexico either reflects or rejects this legacy.

Central Part, lower. The Aztec Prince Cuautémoc battles the Conquistador Cortés

Cuautémoc Battles Cortés. Diego Rivera

Central Part, higher.

The figures of the priests Hidalgo and Morelos in the battle for Mexican Independence from Spain in the 19th century. Above them in the central arch: Obregón and Calles, political leaders of the revolution.

Tierra – Libertad. Diego Rivera

Behind the flag saying "Land and Freedom" are Carrillo Puerto, the Indian Socialist Governor of Yucatán, Francisco "Pancho" Villa the Hero of the 1920 Revolution, and Luis Cabrera, the communist agrarian leader who was assassinated.

The Vertical Secondary Panels

In one place is what appears to be almost a caricature (it reminds of the style of Goya) of the Spaniards, especially of Cortés, as deformed or perverted. It shows the evil treatment of the natives during colonial times emphasizing the "Encomienda" and the "Repartimiento."

To the Right: The Reform and Benito Juárez and Padre Bartolomé de las Casas, the first a legitimate indigenous President of Mexico of Zapotec lineage, the second the great defender of the natives during the Conquest. Below are scenes from pre-revolution days: the "rurales" or rural police and a workers' strike. Note that Frida Kahlo, one of Rivera's wives, is depicted as a young heroine.

To the Left: The Regime of Dictator Porfirio Díaz of 1910. Also the figures of Emiliano Zapata, Otilio Montaño, Carranza and Vasconcelos.

Panel to the right and the stairway

This panel represents a utopic vision of Mexico prior to the Conquest. The legendary pre-Hispanic god-king Quetzalcóatl, creator of culture, civilization and knowledge, is found serenely seated amongst his vassals. Images of the cultivation of the land and the old sculptures are to the side.

Rivera also included another aspect of this world of battles and slavery: human sacrifice to the gods. One sees an Aztec priest brandishing an obsidian knife in one scene; in another, warriors are in the middle of intertribal conflict. But the panel is meant to be free of judgment about the Indigenous peoples. Rivera chose to depict myth, legend and superstition. In the upper part of the second level there appears a feathered serpent which comes out of a volcano amongst tongues of fire. On the right Quetzalcóatl appears seated in a serpent-canoe departing from the Indigenous world, expulsed by the natives themselves, those to whom he had taken civilization and knowledge. There are no trappings of morality or faith; the painter works making no judgments.

The scenes are many: a street scene of life in Tenochtitlán, a tattooed Indian lady of the "Great Tenochtitlán," scenes of weaving, the nobility of warriors viewing women's arts, a scene from "El Tajín" depicting an encounter of warriors from the Totonac Civilization, and the growing of corn and the use of the "metate" from the Huastec Culture.

Panel to the Left and the Stairway

"Mexico Today and Tomorrow," the struggle of Mexican workers and the Marxist solution

There are images of contemporary Mexican workers – peasants, miners, rural school teachers, students and members of Marxist workers unions. In the center are the roots of all evil power: foreign capitalism, the military, evil politicians and the Catholic Church. To the right one sees the workers' strikes and above Karl Marx is speaking for the union of worker, soldier and peasant to abolish private property, class division and to form a new society.

I told Amy, "There is a lot to say about all it. I took pictures of it all and your advertising people can decide what to emphasize. To a traveler or adventurer it will be overwhelming, particularly if they know little of the history of Mexico. Rivera did not do it for us but for Mexicans who have studied all these things in school and are never allowed to forget any of it. The Marxist View will shock our travelers and maybe repel them, but the truth is that this is the ideological basis of what has driven Mexico since 1917 – the Revolution throwing off the vestiges of Spain's colonization and upper class and church rule ever since.

"I think they will appreciate the murals in the sense of painting. Don't misunderstand me, but this is Mexico's small version of the palace nobility and dare I say Vatican painting in Europe. The winners do the paintings and the "frescos," not the losers, and these were in the winners in 1917.

Amy said, "I agree this cannot be overlooked for the expedition. Stunning and maybe a bit depressing though. What's next Mike?"

THE METROPOLITAN CATHEDRAL OF MEXICO

"Another entire chapter of Mexico, stunning as well, maybe depressing as well if one knows the entire story. The National Cathedral or as they call it "La Catedral Metropolitana de la Ciudad de México.""

Metropolitan Cathedral, Mexico City

The church has a long and a very convoluted history, but suffice to say, it also is the "History of Mexico" from Hernán Cortés and conquest days to the present. Amy and I agree that this was all becoming too much, even for an abbreviated trip brochure and we would have to place three or four good books as pre − trip reading for adventurers and travelers. I immediately voted for one from the Ph.D. program: "Many Mexicos" by Lesley Bird Simpson, imminently readable for our purposes.

The Cathedral started as a small church shortly after Cortes's time and gradually becoming the behemoth it is today. It was constructed by the Spaniards from stones of the destroyed Aztec Temples, notably the Temples of Quetzalcóatl and Huitzilopochtli (the Sun God), in today's terms, a desecration of history! Upon its completion after 250 years of work, it rivals the great churches of Spain, of Sevilla and Toledo, modeled upon them. From the Gothic to the Renaissance, to the Baroque and to the Mexican "piled higher and deeper" version of the latter, the Churrigueresque, it has it all. Five naves, a couple of dozen chapels that are churches in themselves. I told Amy my introduction was a Sunday morning mass in 1962 with just a few dozen people attending, hard wooden, worn kneelers, unintelligible Spanish from a lousy p.a. system, mainly women and children in attendance, and most memorable of all: the few men in attendance who walked outside during the sermon to smoke!

Coming from a fresh undergraduate education with the Jesuits in Kansas City in 1962 I only had a vague idea of Mexican History, and certainly not the life and death struggles and battles in the 20th century. No less than Diego Rivera's "History of Mexico," this cathedral building complex with all its secrets encompasses all Mexico. Our AT and NYTT people had to at least do what we Catholics used to call "a short visit." One is in effect simply overwhelmed while sitting on an old pew and looking at the immensity, silver and gold guilt altars blackened by years of incense and candle smoke. I can see why the Protestants of the world would recoil in shock. We took a deep breath, walked out into the bright sunlight of the Plaza and then took a taxi to the final stop this morning, "El Palacio de Bellas Artes."

Bellas Artes, Mexico City

Just down the street from the Zócalo on Alameda is the beautiful, all marble "Palacio de Bellas Artes" started by old dictator Porfirio Díaz in 1905 (the Revolution intervened until 1917, the "Cristero" War of the 1920s, so it was not finished until the 1930s). It is the national concert hall for orchestra and the "Balé Folclórico de Mexico," but for AT and NYTT people it's the top two floors filled with some of the best murals of ALL the painters of the Revolution, Rufino Tamayo, Diego Rivera again but with a different and important work: "Man at the Crossroads". The latter has an amazing story: it was actually commissioned by the Rockefellers in New York, man coming into the industrial age. But when Diego refused to remove the image of Vladimir Lenin, the Rockefellers balked and so did Diego anew and the image was destroyed. But the Riveras had taken pictures; Diego would reproduce it for Bellas Artes years later. David Siqueiros and José Clemente Orozco are there as well, thus the "big four" of government sponsored public art of the Revolution.

Of note on the main floor, the concert hall, is the famous stained - glass curtain and its subject "The Valley of Mexico." It is said to be composed of one million individual pieces of colored stained glass ordered from Tiffany's in New York. Amy and I spent an hour that morning, awed once again by Mexico and its history and art. We agreed and had no trouble adding it to the "must" list for the trip.

This time we took a "regular" taxi back through heavy traffic to our hotel, ate a light lunch, had a quick nap and psyched ourselves up for a long afternoon, turning out to not be nearly so taxing as that long a.m. Alberto picked us up and we drove now all the way south to University City of the National University of Mexico (UNAM) and then to nearby Coyoacan to check out the Frida Kahlo – Diego Rivera houses.

I was jabbering to Amy in the van, telling my tales of the summer of 1962 when I took a city bus most days (and a "pesero" on others) all the way to the UNAM for summer classes in language which I dropped and instead took two amazing literature classes by professors as fine as I've ever experienced. One was this very classy "profesora" who taught "La Novela Picaresca" of Spain and I innocently, naively, got myself into a "tight spot:" choosing "Guzmán de Alfarache" for my paper and report, "the best of the novels," she said. And one thousand pages. Did I skip some pages? Not many. Maybe I would have gotten around Mexico City more if I had chosen the 150 - page famous "Lazarillo de Tormes." The other class was night and day and amazing: a "Catedrático" [Full Professor] from the UNAM who taught us "Works of Cervantes Other than the 'Quixote,'" lecturing in Oxford English. I used his notes at U. of N. in the Survey of Spanish Literature course.

The UNAM then had over 100,000 students, THE university to open doors, get ahead and participate in Mexican politics, especially the Law School. It was and still is a political hotbed, the students the first to protest major national and international events. This time was no exception. Socialist President Allende in Chile had just been overthrown by a military coup d'état and a General named Augusto Pinochet was named "interim" president. It was widely held and accurately so that the coup was "aided and abetted" by no less than the CIA. If you know anything about Mexico – U.S. History and diplomatic relations it's easy to see the turmoil. Alberto herded us away from the demonstrations. On the other side of the huge campus where I even then in 1962 walked by and never entered was one of the most phenomenal of all Mexican buildings – the library covered on all sides by mosaic tiles. Adventurers would get tired of Amy and me calling it "Yet another of the marvels of Mexico." Built from 1950 to 1956, all four walls are covered with the tile mosaics depicting once again "The Cultural History of Mexico." I think one would have to stand outside the building with binoculars and a guide to figure it all out, but just the same we had to see it. In an aside, not necessarily apropos of the moment, Amy wondered if I met any cute Mexican girls. Lamentably enough, or not, I was in with all the Americans in the summer school and am sure I did not impress several dates because of my very "low budget" offerings. Amazingly enough we made it to a couple of good restaurants, the "Baroque" movie houses of Mexico on Insurgentes and Reforma (I think admission was less than a dollar), and that one night on top of the María Isabel. "We're doing a lot better now, huh?"

After university city Alberto drove us through traffic to Coyoacán and to "The Blue House," the house where Frida Kahlo was born, raised and lived much of her life, (1907 to 1954) including intervals with now – on, now – off husband Diego Rivera. Their tempestuous relationship was made famous throughout Mexico. There's too much to say and I don't know what's important for our adventurers. Just a few facts: Frida and Diego were both devout Marxists until their deaths, Diego juggling his beliefs and philosophy with his mostly Capitalist patrons, including Nelson Rockefeller in New York. Frida, crippled by polio, recovered, and then was a victim of the trolley car accident experiencing years of recovery and surgeries, and in chronic back pain until her death. It was the long period of recuperation from the trolley car wreck when she began painting, almost all self-portraits. She was just beginning to become known as an artist in her own right and not just Diego Rivera's lover – wife in my days of 1962. And there was the "interim" of Leon Trotsky who lived with them for over two years, always in fear of assassination by Stalin, but with time to be attracted to Frida for a tryst and then his own falling out over Marxist ideology with Diego.

Amy and I agreed that both the library and the Blue House had to be on the adventurer itinerary. I found the Blue House to be a bit overwhelming because of the hundreds of objects of Mexican folklore, all the art studio stuff and the number of paintings of her own art collection, with just a few of her own and Diego's (not the main ones; they were in museums or the houses of very rich people). Amy said we could put it in the itinerary, make it an option and see what happens. Okay.

That night I took Amy to another of Mexico City's "tourist" places, "Las Delicias" not too far from Reforma. I would not call it a "tourist trap," but it indeed was on the "circuit." Well deserved in my opinion for the Mexican cuisine (including a thick onion and cheese soup) but especially for the show of Mexican music and dancing. I recall especially the "La Jarocha" harp music and Jalisco favorites. Adventurers would possibly one day discover my weakness in Mexico – after a couple of Dos Equis and local music, Gaherty was always a happy camper, ready to sing and dance and play guitar. Amy, with much more real-world culinary experience, wondered if we should check out "fine dining" in D.F. Search me! Tomorrow we start the real Pre-Columbian archeological sites and no better place than Teotihuacán!

6

PRE – COLUMBIAN MEXICO

TEOTIHUACÁN

As we got in the van and pulled away from the María Isabel, Alberto warned us, "You are going to see the other Mexico this morning and I am not talking about the ruins. This is the part of D.F. we are not proud of." I said, "Alberto, we both have traveled a lot in the so – called 'Third World' – Amy more than I. I've seen the 'favelas' in Rio and so has she. I admit I led a sheltered life here in D.F. in 1962 as a student. My host family drove me out to Teotihuacán and I don't remember the scenery. Just let us know what you are thinking."

"Nada Profesor! Gracias. We will be going through a vast area of slum housing with minimal sanitary conditions and often without water. It is crime ridden, and the people struggle just to survive. The government has the best of intentions to improve their lot, but is overwhelmed. My own view, not too Mexican Catholic – massive instruction and birth control years ago would have helped. But you know that "machismo" is alive and well in this country and that includes the poorest of the poor."

I won't dwell on it. We were on a four-lane asphalt divided highway, not a freeway; we passed mile after mile of perhaps the most depressing living area I had ever experienced. Shacks, dirt streets, abandoned cars, but with people in those streets. I was shocked to see a road sign or bill board we

56

might call it, and its message says it all: "Di 'no' al suicidio." ["Say 'no' to suicide."] I could not believe my eyes; this was a first. Amy saw it too and said "We've got to talk about this tonight in the hotel. I lived for one full year in Rio and saw the poverty but Porra! Miguel! It's green and there are banana trees and greenery in the 'favelas.' This makes me want to cry."

"Me too Amy. When I left Brazil in 1967 the first time to come home, we came via Lima and I saw the "pueblos jóvenes" (the massive slums - that's a euphemism if I've ever heard one!) There is no vegetation; it was like this and it affected me. I've never wanted to go back to Lima. Alberto, just a question, is this the only way to get to Teotihuacán?"

"Señor Miguel, sí y no. You can go all the way around through San Miguel de Allende and then back south to the north entrance, but that will take three hours in traffic. Don't you think your travelers should not be blindfolded but see what Mexico offers them? I've been assisting Roberto Maya for a long time and this is not the first time we've had to deal with this. I suspect any major U.S. city would offer the same." "Alberto, you're right, but not like this, I mean on this scale! I know it took decades if not a century for the rural migration from all over Mexico to the D.F. and 'opportunity' in the big city to create this. But the results are shocking." We did soon pass those suburbs, traveled just a few miles through dry land, some irrigated and the grandeur of Teotihuacán was before us. Teotihuacán was huge and dry (still at the end of the dry season in the Valley of Mexico), a bit stark; there was no green or trees as I had seen after Mexico and in Guatemala in 1962.

I'm repeating some information from the Anthropology and History Museum in Mexico, necessary I think to jog travelers' minds. The entire site is known as "The place of those who have the roads to the gods" or "The place where men became gods" – these were the names the Aztecs used to describe the place seven centuries after the apogee of Teotihuacán. This was perhaps the first great "Tollán – Place of the Reeds." It is the proto-culture of central Mexico.

The city-center thrived from 150 A.D. to 650 A.D. It, in effect, was the "metropolis" of the Valley of Mexico with 125,000 people at its height. Seven hundred years after its demise the Aztecs in Tenochtitlán would make pilgrimages to the site under their leader Moctezuma II!

The center was founded or based on two gods: "la Gran Diosa" or "Great Goddess," a feminine god, and the God of Storms. (Amy and I became believers.) Originally the center was related to a cult coming from a cave; from that cult they developed the Temple of the Moon (150 A.D.) and then the Temple of the Feathered Serpent (Quetzalcóatl) in 200 A.D. and finally the Temple of the Sun in 225 A.D.

At its high point, Teotihuacán had contacts with the Maya in the South – at Kaminaljuyú near today's Guatemala City in the highlands and at Tikal in the lowlands. It was burned and sacked in 650 A.D. and the inhabitants migrated or fled to other nearby areas, including Tula. Around 600 A.D. it was the sixth city in the world in size. Constantinople at the same time was larger with some 600,000 population.

We spent at least two or three hours of hard physical exercise walking the length of the main "avenue," interrupted by up and down rock stairways, seeing and climbing the stairways of the three major temples, always anticipating what our adventurers would want to see. As you enter the site the immense pyramid of the Sun is in front of you. We stood in awe at its immensity, but since it is in the center of the archeological zone, we would see the "Street of the Dead" and The Temple of Quetzalcóatl first, come back to the Pyramid of the Sun and finish with the Pyramid of the Moon.

La Calle de los Muertos

This name comes from the Aztecs of later times. It runs on the way to the "Recinto de Quetzalcóatl" or "District of Quetzalcóatl," via the north-south axis. Along the "Calle de los Muertos" there were small temples and/or tombs. The street climbs or descends due to construction and rock stairways. When one walks on the Calle toward the Temple of Quetzalcóatl, the Temple of the Sun is to the left; the Temple of the Moon is behind you.

Templo de Quetzalcóatl

This temple celebrates and commemorates warfare; they have found 300 skeletons, supposed victims of human sacrifice on a large scale. And to one side is what is called the Temple of Quetzalcóatl – He of the Plumed or Feathered Serpent. ("Quetzal" is the sacred bird of the Maya and much of southern Mexico. Much more on them later.) The heads of the Feathered

Serpents (they line the stairways) weigh more than four tons each and were originally painted in blue, red, white and yellow colors. This difficult name has already come up two or three times and it's time to address it. I've spent hours, weeks and months studying this stuff. The legend grows, is modified or contested constantly by scholars.

Quetzalcóatl is at the center of legend, myth and perhaps reality in much of Mexican Pre – Columbian history. One theory, already very briefly mentioned, was that the Toltecs (think: Tula, then the region around Lake Texcoco in the Valley of Mexico, then Chichén – Itzá in the Yucatan) originated somewhere around Cuernavaca, had a king named Mixcóatl, and then another man – king – god named Quetzalcóatl. Of more import is a second legend associated with the Toltecs in the city – site of Tula near old Teotihuacán. There is a fact: the Toltecs did indeed live in Tula for more than two hundred years, and probably lived in a resurged area near the old abandoned Teotihuacán (650 A.D.) taking on much of the religion and culture of its scattered survivors. In their version of the myth Quetzalcóatl is a God (thus the Aztec names for the center centuries later, "the place where men became gods"), the god of goodness and the god who gave knowledge and corn, the staple of all life, to the Toltecs. At the same time there was a dark god of evil, Tezcatlipoca, god of the night and rival of Quetzalcóatl. Tezcatlipoca according to legend got Quetzalcóatl inebriated and told him he had committed incest with his own sister; he then became so ashamed that he fled Tula to the east to the Gulf of Mexico, and either was immolated in fire becoming the Morning Star Venus or left on a raft of reeds in the ocean to the east, vowing someday to come back to his people and restore the kingdom.

It does not stop there: Quetzalcóatl became "Kukulcan" the feathered serpent in the resurgent Maya – Toltec Civilization at Chichén – Itzá in the Yucatan (based on a late Maya group called the Itzáes and Toltecs migrating from Tula). And it gets more complicated: there is evidence of a feathered serpent god as far back as the early Olmecs in the Isthmus of Tehuántepec. I'm sorry I brought it up! Finally, the Aztecs when they migrated from the north and west of Mexico and arrived in the Valley of Mexico in the 14th century adopted and adapted the legend of Quetzalcóatl into their own religion and a major temple, round in nature, was dedicated to him in their capital Tenochtitlán. So this temple in ancient Teotihuacán is dedicated to the same man – god.

The Pyramid of the Sun

La Pirámide del Sol

It stands 61 meters high and is constructed on top of a cave or primitive underground cult site. There are five platforms or levels, a central stairway which divides as you ascend, and becomes one stairway up on top. Scholars are not in agreement as to the exact cult celebrated at the top of the pyramid, but think it was perhaps dedicated to the God of Storms or The Great God. When Amy and I were standing on the flat top a terrific wind and rain storm came up. We had rain equipment but were still soaked, and I daresay, shaken! We got down on hands and knees and crawled to the stairway, then ever so carefully worked our way down those slick steps to the bottom, breathed a sigh of relief and joked "Maybe that Water Goddess in the Museum in Mexico City really was wringing water out of her 'huipil or 'blouse.'" Should we leave Mexico for the Mexicans? I do add that at least there was no lightning or thunder up on top, just wind and rain. That was enough. God of Storms. Hmm.

We noted that many of our adventurers and travelers would be retired people, some in their 70s, some not always up to steep stairways. That indeed would be a factor in our trip planning. Teotihuacán was just the first case of tall pyramids and far from the last. Amy said there are always notices in the trip brochures, i.e. "This trip entails strenuous exercise, many climbs on staircases of pyramids, temples and the like" or something to that effect. We left it for now. One more pyramid or temple to go – that of the Moon.

The Pyramid of the Moon

La Pirámide de la Luna.

It was dedicated to what they call "The Great God" with her power coming from Cerro Gordo (the volcanic mountain behind the pyramid). Guides noted the "harmony of the outline of the mountain to the rear and the pyramid itself," i.e. that is, the pyramid was constructed, it is believed, to imitate nature (a similar phenomenon in Monte Albán and other Mesoamerican sites.) In 1972 there was on – going construction, and scientists were discovering that like other pyramids throughout most of Mesoamerica, there are continuous new constructions, one atop another as rulers come and go. One curious aside – a guide noted that supposedly Frida Kahlo brought Leon Trotsky to the Pyramid of the Moon during their brief but intense love – courtship. I asked Amy, "Am I your misplaced Irishman? Ha!"

In truth, we were now exhausted and hungry as well. Alberto took us to a touristy restaurant nearby where the food was good, the beer icy cold and with Mexican Marimba music to boot, the place a bit "over the top" with "Mejicanidad" but Amy thought a welcome respite for us and the travelers to come. As we were met with very rude and greedy comments from the Marimba player, Amy scratched this place off the "possible" list. Remember we are in effect traveling "incognito" and local hotels and restaurants are only included in the plan if Amy (and I) think they are possible and pleasant, and always after the fact.

As we ended that intense visit to at least one of the cradles of Pre – Columbian Civilization in Mexico, there were still questions. There is still a debate going on concerning the following: did the same ethnic group found and build both Teotihuácan and then Tula? We know the name given to the peoples of Tula is the Toltecs (of later fame both at Chichén-Itzá in the Yucatán and in the Valley of Mexico as antecedents to the Aztecs). My conclusion drawn from a reading of many sources is that the people who founded Teotihuacán were a distinct ethnic group than the Toltecs, who indeed only came 500 years later than the founding of Teotihuacán. However, the cult to Quetzalcóatl, later to be found throughout Mexico, was first in evidence at Teotihuacán.

So far so good, I was providing the background on the history and culture of the project, Amy a very fast learner challenging me (and the local guides) often with questions. One can rightfully conclude: there is much to be learned and no one agrees. There, I've said it. That's the reason for the myriad series of "Mystery" books on Mesoamerica.

LA VILLA DE GUADALUPE

On the way back into the city, now mid- - afternoon, I convinced Alberto to face traffic and take us to the Villa de Guadalupe, "home" of course to the most famous lady in Mexico, the Virgin of Guadalupe. And "Mother" to most Mexicans. It would be an unforgettable memory of our project and tour.

The short version: this is the Blessed Virgin Mary who appears to a poor Indian in 1531 on top of a hill on the outskirts of Mexico City, the hill called Tepeyac. Juan Diego, as per her instructions, notifies the local archbishop of their meeting and her message she wants a church built to commemorate the occasion; the clergyman does not believe Juan Diego and asks him to ask her for proof. After a series of mishaps, finally on her fourth appearance, Juan returns again to the archbishop, this time with his shawl ("tilma") with roses wrapped in it provided by the Virgin. When he opens it for the Bishop, the roses are gone but the image of the Virgin remains. The rest is history, today the most important religious belief and phenomenon in Mexico and many places beyond.

The Spaniards they are clever! They build a shrine at the place of the appearance (on top of an Aztec shrine dedicated to their main female deity, Tonantzin, the Mother of the Gods). This action did not harm the chances of the Indians' mass belief and conversion to Spanish Roman Catholicism and the Virgin of Guadalupe the Mother of God. The original small church was joined by a large one beginning in 1695, but now at the bottom of the hill, and eventually declared a Basilica as a result of the many miracles attributed to Mary.

I told Amy I saw the original Basilica in 1962, one side slowly sinking into the soil of the emptied Lake of Texcoco, the region taken from the Aztecs and becoming Mexico City. My memories are nebulous: the smell of meat cooking at outdoor food stands, dancers in Indigenous costume performing in the huge atrium of the church, dozens of touristy souvenir stands, pickpockets about. I don't recall seeing the relic – the "tilma" encased in glass. It was my first time at a major religious shrine and honestly it seemed far more commercial than religious.

Now in 1973 with Amy we went up the steps to Tepeyac Hill and views of the old basilica down below and through the smog a view of Mexico City. The plaza down below was full of vendors of food, mariachi bands and lots of hustlers. We made our way back down the hill and its steps to the main plaza; after an hour or so we tired of the crowds, the smell, the noise, the very non-religious atmosphere, met Alberto and were taken through major traffic back to the hotel.

Along Reforma the traffic came to a halt – a noisy demonstration against the coup in Chile and the military regime freshly installed. There were banners with anti – U.S. slogans – "La C.I.A. de nuevo! Bajo los Estados Unidos!" But police controlled the traffic flow allowing the protestors in the middle of the street. We arrived just perhaps thirty minutes later than planned. There was a planned last meeting with Roberto Maya the next morning at 10 and we had reservations at 3:00 p.m. on Mexicana for the city of Oaxaca.

Yet that night it was Amy's call saying we had to investigate a "fine dining" restaurant in Mexico City "just in case" the trip itinerary would call for it. It had to be the top of the Torre Latinaomericana, 39 stories up, earthquake proof, a view of the volcanoes surrounding Mexico City (on a good day) and prices to match the thin air (not "transparent" as Carlos Fuentes wrote). Yours truly experienced escargot for the first time, shared a bottle of fine French wine, and ate something fancy in rich sauce which did not satisfy my hunger. "Is this what fine dining is all about? No wonder all those rich people look like they could fit into their high school prom tuxedos and dresses fifty years later!" Amy reminded me that we enjoyed very similar food several times on "Adventurer" in Brazil and she didn't hear any complaints from me then, so why now? "You're not on the farm in Nebraska any more. Adventurer (and NYTT travelers) will enjoy this spot. Have another glass of wine and see if your disposition improves!" It did; the scenery on that night was spectacular, the candlelight dinner delightful and mainly the company. We topped it off with some private intimate time at the María Isabel. "Is this what a honeymoon is like?" I asked. "Perhaps, did you have something on your mind?" "Uh, no, just wondering, but it's food for thought.

7

TYING UP LOOSE ENDS IN MEXICO CITY AND ON TO OAXACA

I neglected to say that traffic and congestion in the city were even worse because D.F. is preparing for the 1974 Olympics. Amy was concerned this would really mess up any air and hotel reservations for AT and NYTT. On the other hand, national and local security would be ramped up to a high level, thus assuring better safety for travelers, or not? Knowing Mexico, it would be fertile opportunity for the Left and Ultra - Nationalists − a huge worldwide audience! It is Spring 1973, advertising and nuts and bolts for any trip take a few months, so summer 1975 may be the ticket. We'll see.

The other item was setting up one or two lectures on Mexican Culture as added options. One would be for the "high" culture with great possibilities: Poet − Philosopher − Nobel Prize Winner Octavio Paz, Historian and Free Market Capitalist Enrique Krause and Left − of − Center Avant Garde novelist Carlos Fuentes. It would be a "coup" if we could get these luminaries all together; lots of fireworks would ensue. The other would be on Mexican popular culture, just as rich but in another way: the "corridos" or ballads of the Mexican revolution and the "calaveras" and woodcuts of José Guadalupe Posada. It would come down to luck and to see who and what was available. I know that Bellas

Artes is used for such major events. I envisioned a combination lecture – performance – exposition maybe even at Bellas Artes. The rub would be convincing Mexican officials of the wisdom of tying it into even a partial venue for American travelers.

It was becoming apparent that Mexico City just offered "too much" and we would have to pick and choose to include cultural possibilities in the three days of the itinerary. Maybe increase to four days? Lectures and art would be at night; we would have to coordinate with dinner out for the adventurers. Something would have to give. These were just thoughts Amy and I discussed at breakfast that morning before a scheduled meeting with Roberto Maya. While we were at breakfast a call came in and Amy took it. She said Roberto asked if we could make it an hour later. That would really put the crunch on for the flight to Oaxaca but it could be done.

So Alberto picked us up and then pulled up to the office on Insurgentes, but with a surprise. The front display window was entirely boarded up, just with the door open. Roberto was at his desk, a bit disheveled, but bade us sit down. The office was a mess with file cabinets, bookcases and even furniture out of place. "Mike and Amy, this is a first. When we got here this morning this is what greeted us – the street side display window shattered, broken glass all over the office. We're just now getting it cleaned up. I'm just glad it was not two hours later when I and Yolanda (my secretary) would be here. I'm calling it vandalism for now. You know I handle all kinds of tour ventures in Mexico, your AT is just one of them. And this for twenty years. I have close ties with the Ministry of Tourism; we work together and they often have requests for special groups they want to sponsor and see the best of Mexico. The rest is in this note which was tied to a very large brick thrown through the window and found on the floor:

> *Basta con los esfuerzos a vender nuestro país a los efeminados cabrones de afuera que parecen hacer una nueva invasion a nuestro querido México. Nosotros somos pocos y pequeños, 'Los de Abajo', pero juramos hacer todo*

dentro de nuestro poder a estorbar tus esfuersos a arruinar nuestro 'Mexico Querido.' Este es solamente el primer paso, pequeño como nosotros, pero seguramente no el último. Para que sepan: XOLOTL – Protector del Sol Huitzilopochtli en su jornada por la noche, Venus la Estrella de la Noche y Guía a Quetzalcóatl su gemelo

Roberto said, "I'm trying to think how you say it in English, "unbalanced" or "deranged." I think – "desequilibrado" we say. I think Señor "Xolotl" is on the fringe! You know Spanish so you see how he signed the note. "Xolotl" has a half dozen meanings in our mythology, from a "sick" person, to a dog, to the twin of Quetzalcóatl but without any of his positive attributes, a protector of his brother. He's also associated with fire and lightning and a guide in the underworld after death. So who knows exactly what in this case, but probably a "protector" of Mexico from outsiders. You remember our initial conversation, and things have not changed. I advise going ahead with your travel and research; Alberto tells me you are off to a terrific start and this potentially is one terrific trip for AT! I'll keep in touch by phone, and remember, if there is anything unusual, Jaime Torres of the PF is always around. He has already been notified of this incident. Crime, break – ins, and such things are an everyday event in this metropolis of twenty million people."

Amy and I agreed but reluctantly, saying we were set for the 3:00 p.m. Mexicana flight to Oaxaca, but would be in touch regularly. Alberto ran us directly out to the airport where with a one-hour delay; we had plenty of time to review the trip so far and recent events.

After we had checked in and were reading our notes in the waiting room no less than Jaime Torres of the PF came up, politely reintroduced himself and offered to buy us a celebratory drink before Oaxaca. We sat in the Mixcóatl Lounge and had a short conversation. He led off, "Mike y Amy, we have accompanied you, at a discreet distance of course, and you are to be congratulated for an astounding four intense days of seeing the best of Mexico City for your upcoming travelers. I have had the pleasure of working throughout our entire Republic and I daresay your choices of sightseeing, thus far, have been excellent. I am originally from the city of Oaxaca so I can guarantee you wonderful days ahead. I do wish to inform you that there was word from an "informant," let us say, of that unspeakable, cowardly attack on Roberto Maya's office this morning. This reprehensible Mexican who calls himself Xolotl is known to us, is under surveillance, and although we do not have direct proof of this morning's shameful action, I can assure you it will not happen again. Our officers, as we speak, have surrounded his hovel in one of the shanty towns, and he will soon be under arrest for civil violence and removed from further contact with you or with other Mexicans. I hope that reassures you that we of the PF are serious and secondly that your continued research will lead to a wonderful conclusion."

I spoke before Amy, "Gracias, Officer Torres. We appreciate the good work. Just one minor correction if I may, although you have termed our efforts as 'sightseeing,' I would prefer the term 'research;' a minor point but seeing it as more appropriate to our backgrounds, professions and efforts in Mexico. It would indeed be wonderful if we touched base again in Oaxaca for a drink, maybe in the main plaza, and could then catch up on our new adventures."

"Mike, it depends on assignments and needs here, but I assure you I would welcome the opportunity. And you Miss Carrier, we are highly impressed with your knowledge of high-level travel and your choices thus far for your travelers. I hope they bring their pocketbooks! (and he laughs)."

"Thank you, Jaime; we are just getting started, but I can say in all honesty that Mexico City is truly unique in our great world of travel combining a great past and presence. We both look forward to Oaxaca and the Zapotec – Mixtec cultures, the city itself and on to the land of the Maya."

Jaime stood up, offered a formal handshake to both of us and thanked us for our appreciation of PF efforts. A good man to have on your side! The call came for our flight and in thirty minutes we were in the air for the two-hour flight to another world – Oaxaca! We went over our tentative itinerary list, both deciding from everything we had heard that we needed a naturalist birder and / or an animal – birder to fly in to check out a one or two day excursion for birding in the wet forests southwest of Oaxaca down to the ocean. This was an important "gateway" city in itself with some amazing sites, and then the investigation of our second major pre – Columbian culture: Monte Albán and Mitla.

8

OAXACA, MONTE ALBÁN, MITLA, RETURN TO OAXACA

The city is at an altitude of 5070 ft., more than 500 kilometers to the SE of Mexico City. It is the area of the lands of the ancient Zapotecs and their capital of Monte Albán. Oaxaca is a city of fine colonial architecture (24 churches) and the birthplace of Benito Juárez, the first full blooded Indian president of Mexico, a famous "liberal" of the 19th century (more on this very soon).

What a change from Mexico City! The airport at Oaxaca was maybe one -tenth the size, with lots of open areas between the glassed – in single terminal. We grabbed our bags and took a taxi to the city center to one of Amy and AT's splurges – the Camino Real Hotel not far from the famous Oaxaca downtown plaza.

El Hotel Camino Real, Oaxaca

The Camino Real Hotel was originally a spectacular old convent dating from 1574, the Convent of Santa Catalina de Sienna. It was taken over by Benito Juárez and the government in the 1800s. There are a couple of things to know about Júarez: he was full blooded Zapotec, the first Indigenous president of Mexico. He ramrodded the "Second battle of Independence" from Napoleon III and Prince Maximilian in Mexico in the 1860s. But he also was an extreme Liberal in the Liberal – Conservative conflicts of Mexico in the 19th century (civil power over church power, surviving the War of Reform and the French Invasion in cahoots with Mexican Conservatives). Although raised and tutored by priests of the Catholic Church (a lay Franciscan, Benito being urged to go to seminary) he became one of the Church's most important critics and opponents. Juarez's liberal laws outlawed the convent and the nuns (and were an early indication for what would happen after the Mexican Revolution in 1917). So, the convent became a government building, then a jail, then a school, and finally the government palace of Oaxaca. It was made into a hotel in 1972. The walls are the originals, thick up to two meters, with gardens, patios, flowers, and an old basin where the nuns washed clothes.

Led by Amy we took a good look around the hotel and its grounds that late afternoon - cocktails at "Las Bugambilias Bar" (spectacular and in bloom when we were there), overlooking the interior patio with ancient fountain and the 16th century stone walls of the convent. More later in coming days. Immaculately cared for inside and out, it was far more to my and our taste than the big city glass tower of the María Isabel, fit as it was for Mexico City.

We followed the suggestion of the concierge at the hotel to take the short walk to the Zócalo or main plaza for the early evening activity. Advice well taken! I'll say more about it when we begin our itinerary and research for Oaxaca in the morning, but suffice to say it was delightful. This was for me the quintessential atmosphere of the old plazas of Colonial Mexico and more! The plaza was alive with local families, adults and children, tourists of course, vendors of "chicharrones," an ice cream cart, shoeshine boys, strolling musicians, and artisans selling their wares. We sat for awhile at one of the open-air bars in the columnated sides of the plaza, me with an icy Dos Equis and Amy with a margarita. Amy said this was a "must" for the itinerary and checked it off her list!

After dusk and the beautiful lights of the plaza came on we went upstairs to the famous columnated restaurant on the second floor overlooking the main old plaza for dinner and some of the best music I had ever heard in Mexico (I humbly remind the reader again that I was an amateur classic guitar player and huge fan of the "old" folkloric music of Mexico and its "corridos.") We had a truly fun dinner and we enjoyed a great regional musical group who sang all the old "favorites" for Mike: "La Llorona" and others. The menu was chicken in almond sauce, rice, margarita, and strawberry cheesecake. All good to me and Amy as well. An extra Dos Equis or two had me singing along to the "old favorites" and buying cassetes of all they had to offer!

Amy said, "Gringo Viejo! We better get you to bed, a big day tomorrow." No argument. The room was comfortable in that old style, and quiet! The three − foot thick stone walls took care of the Oaxaca Street noise and the plaza down the way. We both agreed that this was a terrific introduction on our "gira" of Southern Mexico.

Full day one in Oaxaca. After breakfast at the "Refectorio" [The Refectory] (great name; these folks used good sense in adapting the old convent names to the modern hotel) the next morning, to wit: food warmed over coals and good coffee, we walked back to the Zócalo with a long list of "lugares imprescindíbiles" ["must" places] to check out for adventurers. It turned out to be truly amazing in its charm and colonial grandeur.

The Santo Domingo Church

Santo Domingo, Oaxaca

Evidence of the above was Old Oaxaca and the Santo Domingo Church. I rated it "Five Stars" with its gold and stucco. The church was constructed in 1575 through 1611 by the Dominican Order. It served as a military barracks for both sides during the War of the Reform of the 1860s and later in the 1910 Revolution. The interior is noted for its statues and stucco decoration and gold adornments. One notes the gold encased "Capilla del Rosario" and the main altar. In the apse, upon entering, one sees the genealogical tree of the founder of the Order, Domínico de Guzmán. There was something on my mind from studies: Padre Bartolomé de las Casas, defender of the Indians (after his own period as a slave owner in the Dominican Republic), mainly in Guatemala but later in Spain defending the native Americans as "human beings" and to be converted to the "True Faith" only voluntarily (clashing with the massive baptisms of the Franciscans). There is the other side of the story of the Dominicans' original role in the Papal Inquisition and then Torquemada in the Spanish Inquisition.

La Casa de Cortés

Impressive from the outside with its 16th century stone construction was the "Casa de Cortés," but equally important historically. Hernán Cortés, the Conqueror of Mexico and Nueva España, of Tenochtitlán and the Aztecs, in 1521, was named the "Marqués del Valle de Oaxaca" by King Carlos V and received such titles and honors. He took an expedition as far as today's Honduras, passing in Oaxaca. He ordered the house to be built but never lived there.

La Plaza Central (El Zócalo)

El Zócalo, Oaxaca

It was but a short walk from there to the main plaza with all its life. There was a fun market, some Indians but with few in "native costume." We saw vendors of chiles, nogal, beans, and weaving. There was time for beers and a sandwich, and best of all, great little Indian girls selling "chicletes" and "animalitos."

The Mercado de "Abastos"

Amy and I took a taxi to the "Mercado de abastos" which was incredible. We saw two Indian ladies cutting and preparing "Nogal" cactus for a drink or soup. In addition, there was a beautiful flower market, a chile market (one is urged to try "mole oaxaqueño," a variant of "mole poblano." Look out!). We saw a meat market, another sector where they made beautiful "piñatas," and Indian ladies weaving straw articles and mats.

Zapotec Lady and Huipil - Vestido

I escaped to another part to the market and met a Zapotec Indian lady, or a descendant of the same, who showed me a beautiful woven "Huipil-Vestido." After much bargaining in an interesting bilingual conversation: me speaking Spanish to one Indian lady, she translating in an Indian language to the lady who did the weaving, and back and forth, I bought the article for a fair amount of dollars. It would be either a wonderful decoration for the apartment back in Lincoln or a gift to relatives.

Day Two. Oaxaca to Monte Albán

It is Sunday. I have stomach problems. But Pepto helped. Breakfast consisted in pineapple juice, eggs, bread, and hot chocolate. The day began with Amy and I in a contracted van to a viewpoint overlooking Oaxaca and the statue of its native son, Benito Juárez, future anti-liberal president of Mexico and great national hero in the wars against the French. As mentioned earlier, the irony with the great Benito was that he was a poor young child who was educated by the clergy of the Church and later their persecutor. We have Fidel Castro one century later, a product of the elite Jesuit College in Havana who became Latin America's most famous Marxist! From the hill Oaxaca seemed smogged in; we found out it was the annual burning of the corn stalks before harvest. The wind blew it out later.

After the view point, we drove to the west and up another hill to Monte Albán. It is a major Pre – Columbian Site in Mexico, but for different reasons. It began in the Pre-Classic period and lasted a long time, well into the late classic period, thus from 500 B.C. to 400-900 A.D. It was contemporary to Teotihuacán and the beginnings of Tula. After the site of Monte Albán was abandoned by the Zapotecs, the Mixtecs used the place up to the 11th century.

Scholars speak of the harmony between the edifices and the mountains that surround them, of the "stelae," of the similarity to Maya art, and the site as a "microcosmic replica" of the area that surrounds it. Archeologists have found more than 170 tombs (this is the real legacy of the place), altars and stelae at Monte Albán. They also speak of the symmetry of the Acropolis.

Vía Procesional, Monte Albán

Although there is no fixed axis like at Teotihuacán, Monte Albán does remind one somewhat of the "Calle de los Muertos" of the former. There is a "Processional Route" or "Vía Procesional" between the temples, running from north to south; the central plaza is small. The guide says one could place it beneath the Pyramid of the Sun at Teotihuacán. Looking toward the center-south from the "Vía Procesional," they think the building in the form of an arrow head was a sort of observatory because it is off the north-south axis and seems to be placed according to the stars.

Then there is the ball court in the form of the letter I; I'll have much more to say about the "ball game," ubiquitous in southern Mexico and the Yucatán.

The view from the South Platform looks toward the Temple of the "Danzantes" or Dancers. Stelae found at this site are currently in the

Museum of Anthropology in Mexico City, and we already commented on them and saw photos. The stones of "stelae" of the "Danzantes" are in front of the oldest temple in Monte Albán (one notes the slight similarity to the faces of the Olmec heads at La Venta). Many theories, and they are just that, speak of what the "danzantes" really are:

a. They represent babies at birth, infants or dwarfs
b. They all represent men who are dead, naked, and have closed eyes and are victims of war or sacrifice.

A final note: Monte Albán is famous for its tombs, one such described on our tour of the Museum in Mexico City. These tombs were discovered and excavated by the famous Alfonso Caso in the 1930s; they contain "frescos" in the style of Teotihuacán. They also had superimposed sculptures on large ceramic vases. It is believed that the vases contained food for the journey of the deceased to the "other world." Many gold ornaments and objects, a tomb robber's paradise.

Tomb 105, Monte Albán

One of the tombs proved to be the richest tomb of all Mesoamerica with some 500 objects discovered: gold breastplates, jade, pearls, marble, fans, masks, and gold belts with precious stones. This material is in the regional museum of Oaxaca and the Museo Nacional de Antropología in Mexico City.

In the last days of Monte Albán, there was a gradual departure of the Zapotec people, and these peoples moved to other sites in the area, in particular, Mitla. Some two hundred years later, the Mixtec people arrived in Mitla but built no new constructions, and Monte Albán was converted into a necropolis and then a place of pilgrimage.

Maybe it was the hot day or just the total brownness of the place, but we both were not super impressed. Yet one cannot dismiss the Zapotecs and this place (there is proof of their standing and relationship as far back as Teotihuacán); its great importance for the tombs and their riches alone puts it on the list of major Pre − Columbian sites. But we both decided that it would require minimal time in the itinerary, either an a.m. or p.m., not all day.

On our return to Oaxaca, Amy and I went directly to the Plaza, and back to Santo Domingo Church and Rosario Chapel. On some kind of religious "binge" we decided to remember our roots and go to mass in the Oaxaca Cathedral near the plaza. That might have been a mistake; it was not a religious experience perhaps (a favorite archeology word) with a priest officiating that I could not get one word due to the lousy speaker system and echo. There were very few people at mass and there was "youth" folk music. I dozed until communion. Amy and I had not yet an opportunity to really talk about our respective religious situations, although we both knew of each other's Catholic tradition (Irish and French). She had read my accounts of Brazil, sprinkled now and then with references to the Church (but a lot more with African religion, Spiritist religion in Brazil and a few visits to amazing old Catholic churches), and knew of my "evolved" Catholicism. I knew less of her "faith journey," mentioned it, but she said that would have to remain for later. Okay.

We needed something to revive us after that and found it all at that same restaurant – bar in the colonnades of the Plaza – icy beer and a margarita. Both of us were in need of a hot shower and a fresh change of clothes, so it was back to our colonial decorated room at the Camino Real, some intimate time and talk of all we had seen in just two days. There was another archeological site tomorrow – Mitla - and we hoped a leisurely p.m. back in Oaxaca and then a short – hop flight to what would be the most beautiful part of Mexico yet, the city of Tuxtla Gutierrez the capital of Chiapas State and a van to San Cristóbal de las Casas and the world of the Maya, then and now.

One unanswered question and matter was the role of nature on the proposed expedition. Up to now there really was nothing to report, but the hotel concierge waxed euphoric telling us what "massive" amounts and varieties of birds one could find in the jungles and forest of Oaxaca State, just hours south and southwest of the city to the ocean. (Query: was he stirring up business?) Swallowing her pride (and me too) Amy and I actually went to a travel agency specializing in such things. After some talk, we were encouraged to "take just one day with our guide." The fact remains we are not naturalists. This was not according to the AT "Bible." Damn. Buck or Jack or Kelly from "Adventurer" should be here. Amy however said similar circumstances with other trips are commonplace. If we deemed it a possibility, AT would fly someone down for two or three days to check it out, and if good results were found, incorporate it into the plan. Upon further exploration and conversation we discovered the fly in the ointment: you might have to spend as much as seven days to see the endemic species they bragged about (and our proposed trip could spare just one!), but more important, major birding is during the winter migration from the north joining the local species, December to March. The proposed AT – NYTT summer trip would be dicey. We were told that in the higher country, the mountains and forests of Chiapas (and we are now in the dry season) and the rain forest around Palenque would be a better chance. We tabled it.

THE TRIP TO MITLA

On the way we stopped at Santa María del Tule which has the largest "ahuetehuete" tree in Mexico. The tree measures 42 meters in diameter, 43 meters high and is perhaps 2000 years old. Worth the sight!

MITLA

The site dates from Pre-Classic times, its apogee being after the abandonment of Monte Albán, but it was still inhabited at the time of the arrival of the Spaniards in the 16th century. The experts believe the Zapotecs from Monte Albán built the place and inhabited it between 0 and 900 A.D. The Mixtecs arrived later, and at the end there was contact with the Aztecs. In one corner of the site there is a Spanish, Catholic Church; today festivals in the same incorporate both the Spanish and Native rites. The archeological site is small, less than two square kilometers; the name comes from the Náhua "Mictlán," land of the dead. Indigenous people actually lived in the site until 1700 when the Spanish finally took control of the area.

El Palacio, Mitla

A "supreme priest" ruled and there was human sacrifice. He lived in the "Palace" in the "Grupo de las Columnas." On the four sides of the Palace there are large rooms; the walls are decorated on the surface with blocks of stone cut in rectangles, squares and parallelograms, all representing geometric games and are called "The Zapotec Mosaics." This palace was contemporary to the Governor's Palace in Uxmal in the Yucatán, a major late Maya site we will see later, and the interior rooms use the same decoration as that of Uxmal. This connection will be important if my studies are correct. The designs "perhaps" are derived from patterns of textiles of Indian blouses or "huipiles" from the area (or the opposite one might say).

After seeing the archeological site, we had the good fortune to witness an Indian wedding at the local church. I felt we were interlopers, and we were, but the photo I shot tells much of the Zapotec peoples still living in Mitla. The wedding procession later was a marvel to see (we stood quietly behind a cactus fence to witness it). I wish we could have congratulated the bride and groom; it was an honor to witness the important moment from afar.

Casamiento Indio, Mitla

RETURN TO OAXACA

Upon our return to Oaxaca after lunch at the hotel we went to the Rufino Tamayo Museum which was excellent, 5 stars! It had the best ceramics we have seen in Mexico and some stelae as well, and of course the paintings from the master (as already mentioned in Mexico City, one of "the big four" of Mexico's Post -Revolution painters). Amy added it to the list of "possibles" for the adventurers' time in Oaxaca. Once again, like Mexico City, there was a lot to choose from and a process of elimination would have to take place.

There was a bit of relaxation in the main plaza of Oaxaca, an extremely interesting and colorful place, where Mike got a 6 - peso boot shine. There was a place we had missed earlier - the Jesuit "Compañia" Church just to the side of the main plaza with its "miracle room." Of note was an image of Jesus Christ carrying the cross on the "Via Dolorosa," a statue in the old Jesuit church called "La Iglesia de la Compañia." The Jesuits, as I never tire of reminding, were expelled from Latin America in 1767, losing their missions, schools and hospitals. In this case, the old church is to the side of the main plaza, "El Zócalo," in Oaxaca. There was yet another aspect of the church very familiar to me from Brazil, a phenomenon I think throughout the Latino World – I speak of the "miracle room" where people leave "ex -votos" or notes of thanks in the form of a photo of the "healed person" for miracles ceded to them by a saint, the Virgin Mary or Jesus himself. I note that in Brazil they leave Plaster of Paris models of the parts healed – hands, arms, legs, and even heads. Adventurers saw this in Salvador da Bahia on our expedition last year. In this case it was Jesus who did the healing; I've included the slide I took. I saw the same thing in the Church of San Francisco in Antigua in Guatemala.

Jesus, Ex – Votos, Jesuit Church, Oaxaca

Not only does one see the "ex -votos" or photos, but a very Spanish and now Mexican phenomenon: a predilection for the suffering Christ and the splendid clothing the women's groups spend hours making and insisting on placing on the statues. I saw it in Guatemala in the highlands in Maya churches – the Virgin in a 'huipil" exactly like the Maya ladies and Jesus with splendid clothing. Add this place to the "possible" list!

Amy always seemed to have the last item, and tonight was no less memorable than the Torre Latinoamericana Restaurant in Mexico City.

We dined, that's the word, "fine dining" in the Camino Real, and had a last drink in the candle lit bar called "Las Novicias," great name! There was plenty of time to remember the last three days and we both agreed Oaxaca and surrounding ruins were a terrific second chapter to our journey. Amy said a funny thing, "Did you have a special prayer before Jesus in the Jesuit Church, I thought I saw your lips moving. Oh … none of my business."

"Young lady in fact I did. I was thanking Jesus for this amazing time here with you, and more importantly, just you." I barely said that when I was enveloped in a warm embrace, and a long tender kiss. "Gracias Miguel, me tocaste el corazón."

9

ON TO SAN CRISTÓBAL
AND PALENQUE

The next morning we said goodbye to Oaxaca, reluctantly, and boarded a short flight to Tuxtla Gutiérrez, capital of the State of Chiapas. I was really looking forward to the next few days, as was Amy, but me particularly for all the history, the beauty of the mountains as we began to climb out of the capital to San Cristóbal de las Casas, and the rain forest to come later around Palenque. We were now in the heartland of the Mayas.

There was some personal history as usual. In 1962 after school at the UNAM I had taken a bus from Mexico City to the border of Guatemala (riding on the rumble seat over the tire, no air conditioning, no muffler and all the while thinking of Spain's movie director Buñuel's famous "Mexican Bus Ride"). I did see something of Puebla, its church towers and nearly became sick with the winding road. After a horrible sleepless night, I awoke to a scene I'll never forget – Maya men and women in native, woven clothing, walking along the road to an early morning market in Comitán near the border. Lots of cattle, sheep and goats, and green everywhere, this after so much of the dryness of central Mexico. We eventually after much hassle over papers and bus tickets, and I daresay a few bribes, crossed over from Mexico into Guatemala. We boarded a "school bus" like I rode when in grade school in Nebraska, riding now through Maya "milpas" [cornfields], pine forest, and then a treacherous road hugging mountain passes with rivers far below. The road was washed out in several spots and our intrepid driver got out, tramped around, inspected and forged ahead. I remembered all of my old Catholic prayers – St. Michael the Archangel, Angel of God My Guardian Dear, and all the rest. We made it to the highlands of Guatemala and Quetzaltenango where I met my good college friend, Eduardo. That's the memory I shared with Amy as we boarded a van and driver hired by AT for the spectacular drive to San Cristóbal de las Casas, a very famous place.

The van driver insisted we make a stop at a huge reservoir in Sumidero Canyon outside of Tuxtla Gutiérrez and take the boat ride down the lake, promising great scenery and maybe some birds. The lake was impressive, huge and long, at times hugging the canyon walls. Vegetation varied from pines to oak to lots of bushes and trees we could not identify. The birding did not materialize except for dozens of vultures. It is the second largest lake in all Mexico and they like to call it their "Grand Canyon." The Grijalva River creates the reservoir and then flows into the Usumacinta River (important in the Maya area). We were happy to end the ride, get back in the van and began what was spectacular country through Maya villages all the way to San Cristóbal.

The Road to San Cristóbal de las Casas is important both historically and in modern times. We climbed up out of the valley outside of Tuxtla Gutiérrez to the top of the mountain range. It now began to resemble what I expected: "milpas," Maya villages, gardens along the road, pine trees, all very green. Indians were selling weavings along the road. It did not take long to get to San Cristóbal and what all happened later. I'll tell what adventurers would need to know about it first.

SAN CRISTÓBAL DE LAS CASAS

At a little above 7000 ft. San Cristóbal is a colonial city with beautiful and in fact spectacular mountain scenery surrounding it, a land of the descendants of the Maya. In 1524 the Spaniards under Diego de Mazariegos conquered the Indians of the region of what is today's San Cristóbal. They established a city whose original name was "Villareal de Chiapa de Los Españoles," this in 1528. The famous Dominican Friar Bartolomé de las Casas was named Bishop in 1544 and went on to protest the torture, mistreatment and death of Indians in New Spain in his book "Breve Historia de Destrucción de Indias," ("Brief History of the Destruction of Indias"). Violence, the killing of both whites ("ladinos") and Indians has taken place since then. It is said that past and current bishops of the Catholic Church in San Cristóbal, aside from knowledge of the Indians and their language, often are great sympathizers with their cause.

Chiapas was a province of the "Capitanía General de Guatemala" for many years. Because it did not have gold or silver like other parts of New Spain, its importance remained principally as a strategic spot on the border with Guatemala. But due to its rich agricultural lands it became a prime example of the colonial system of the "encomienda" and "repartimiento," (the vehicles for domination of the conquered lands and slave labor of the natives to follow) a factor in its social situation yet today, that is, the treatment of the Indians and their lands.

The principal ethnic groups of the area are the Tzotiles and Tzelales. The common language is Tzotzil (Maya). Chiapas is also the region of the remaining Lacandón Indians; some 450 remain in the eastern part of the state near Palenque and Bonampak, six days' horseback ride from San Cristóbal.

There are precedents to the story of Chiapas: since colonial times there have been struggles and battles to control the land of the natives, always with the involvement of outside interests. Chiapas is an extremely poor state with a high index of alcoholism, hunger, violence, illiteracy and lack of medical treatment. One per cent of the people control 50 per cent of the arable land. In effect the colonial system remains intact. Modern day logging and deforestation (you can imagine the hardwoods taken and disappearing forever) exacerbates the situation. The poverty of the Indians is real and also their simple plea: "We want to govern ourselves; we want to have land to farm and that is our basic human right."

The battle for the defense of the natives goes back to the original conquest and colonization in the 16th century. Its main figure Fray Bartolomé de las Casas, one of the most famous figures of the Spanish Conquest and colony. A priest who originally had his own land and Indians in Santo Domingo in the Dominican Republic, he saw the wide spread abuses of the Spaniards, gave up his own "encomienda" and battled until his death for the rights of the Indigenous of America, especially against the Spanish labor system of the "encomienda." His thoughts are summarized in his already mentioned "Breve Destrucción de Indias." He was instrumental in influencing Spanish King Carlos V of the plight of the natives and the result was the eventual "Nuevas Leyes de Indias" [New Laws of the Indies] in 1542 for justice for the Indians. The problem was they were never totally promulgated and in effect were ignored by most. Las Casas became a Dominican priest, worked in Venezuela and especially in Cobán in Guatemala before being named Bishop in San Cristóbal, originally a part of Guatemala. He was vehemently opposed by Motolinia of the Franciscans for their diverse methods of conversion of the natives and by the well-entrenched Bishop Marroquín of Guatemala. Most important: Las Casas defended the basic tenet that the Indians were human, therefore not subject to forced conversion to the Catholic faith (i.e. slavery); this in the famous Debate of Valladolid in 1550. Briefly Bishop of San Cristobal in 1544 he started the Dominican church and defended the natives. He opposed the Spanish landholders, among them the heavyweight Bernal Díaz de Castillo of Conquest of Mexico fame, saying no confessions were to be granted to landholders and "encomenderos." And last rights only if their Indians were set free and their property returned. Ex-communication if they mis-treated Indians.

The Leyes de Indias were repealed in 1545, there was massive opposition to Las Casas and he was forced to leave San Cristobal in 1546.

He was succeeded in modern days by a Bishop who ruled when Amy and I were in San Cristóbal, Bishop Samuel Ruíz in 1970. He ordered translation of the Bible into Indigenous languages and commissioned all in all 20,000 native catechists to spread the word. He is a worthy successor to Fray Bartolomé in the 1970s. The battles for control of the land and the Indians are still going on during our time there. As tourists you might not notice, but then again.

OUR TRAVELS IN THE AREA

Knowing where to stay was a problem because there were lots of choices, a couple high – end, more in the middle and a few hostel – like for student and budget conscious travelers. The high - end places seemed glitzy and "over the top," more like big city. Amy and I both agreed on a middle range hotel, both for its name and its looks – the Hotel Diego Mazariegos, named after one of the founders and "conquistadores." We liked it because it was near the center of the town, its colonial style blending in with the main style of the old downtown, just a couple of blocks from the Santo Domingo Church, and there were original cobblestone streets on all sides. One interesting note for the mountain climate – there was a "chiminea" in each room, and for $1 they would bring wood each night for a very pleasant small and warming fire in the room. There were embers an hour and one half later. With both of us with some stomach problems, supper that first night was chicken soup, spaghetti and a Lager Oscura Chiapas beer. One minor note to keep in mind: the shower was tiled nicely but the water turned cold in the middle! Amy said adventurers would not like that and we would take the heat! From the adventurers, not the fire. We did notes by the fire and read and talked of the plan for San Cristóbal, to bed and a big day tomorrow!

Oh, a Xolotl update. We had experienced no problems in Oaxaca, but did have a visitor at the hotel in San Cristóbal, an agent of the PF and friend of Jaime Torres. He was seated in the lobby or registration area, not in police uniform but local "tourist" attire. He introduced himself as Pablo Negrete, showed us his badge, and basically gave us an update on the happenings in Mexico City. Lamentably the person called Xolotl had "vanished from the face of the earth; no one from his residence in the north suburbs of Mexico City knows anything about him, Of course, they are his friends, cohorts or relatives. Oh, and Roberto Maya is back in business, the office totally fixed up, and says hello and wishes you a continued good trip. We are keeping track of you and your travel and research, and if there is any need for concern, we will let you know. PF tries to place agents near their home for lots of reasons, not the least, that way each agent knows the territory the best. I am originally from San Cristóbal so can guarantee you there are wonderful things to be seen here; I advise two or three days if you can. My phone is 66 – 696 – 6754, so please let me know if you encounter any difficulties. I do not anticipate any. Oh, I speak two variants of the local Maya language if you need any interpreting. Most local people know some Spanish, particularly those in the markets, so you should be fine. I'm hoping you brought some cash – we here have the most beautiful native weavings in all Mexico as you shall soon see."

"Pablo, thanks for the update. It is disconcerting this Xolotl guy is on the loose, but I suspect he has bigger fish to fry than us. And we are happy Roberto is okay. I think we can do everything in two very busy days, so we hope to be back in the van on our way to Palenque three days from now. We'll give you a quick call to confirm, although I guess you will already know our whereabouts."

Amy piped up a thanks and asked Pablo what did he think of our choice of the Diego Mazariegos? He confirmed there are fancier places, but for genuine local history and atmosphere he would not change a thing. She felt better.

Chamala Indian Lady and Weavings

The next morning after a good breakfast at the hotel, Amy and I went to the weaving market by the Church of Santo Domingo. (We did not take the time to go in but the amazing façade of the church itself was like a Spanish Baroque altar, all carved in stone, very similar to the Church of La Merced I had seen in Antigua, Guatemala back in 1962.) The Tzotzil Indians from San Juan Chamula and several other towns were selling their wares in the large market to the side. We bargained long and hard before each buying a special weaving from San Andrés de Larraínsa, a nearby Maya pueblo. Amy said she had never seen anything like it; I said the same, except in Guatemala, but different. This is the principal market for Indians of the entire region, that is, of the Chamulas (the man's traditional dress is loose pants with white serape, women with a blue "huipil"), of the Zenacantanos (the man's attire is a rose colored shirt, short pants, and a round straw hat with ribbons), and Mayas from Tenahpa (the men wear a black tunic down to the knees and a broad brimmed straw hat).

SAN JUAN CHAMULA

After the market it was back to the hotel for a short van ride to San Juan Chamula an Indian town just a few kilometers along the highway out of San Cristóbal; along the way there was "real" Indian life, weaving, the watering of gardens, a few men hoeing and "plowing" melons. The town is located twelve kilometers north of San Cristóbal and is known for its main church and the syncretism of the Maya-Catholic faith practiced there. There is a brotherhood, "cofradía," which takes care of the church, "those that take care of the saints." There is always someone "on guard" at the church entrance, incidentally with a big club in his hand. Its main festival is during Carnival just before Lent, days which correspond to the final five days of the solar year of the Maya calendar. This calendar and the festival calendar are still used to determine dates in local agriculture.

The church was spectacular! It was much like Santo Tomás in Chichicastenango in Guatemala. The photo shows its façade of white stucco with a red, blue and yellow door with motifs from archeological sites and modern textiles.

San Juan Chamula Church

Interior, San Juan Chamula Church

The photo of the interior, because no flash allowed, is much darker. The interior has no benches or pews; the floor is covered with "Ocosingo" pine needles. Indians pray out loud before "little glass boxes" which contain Catholic saints dressed in a colorful and extravagant manner. The "shamen" or local priests burn candles of various colors, drink Pepsi or Coca Cola as part of the ritual, and may offer eggs or chickens (they supposedly "pass" the sicknesses of the ill to the chickens and the eggs, and these are sacrificed outside the church.)

It was as I've described when all hell broke loose. In the midst of our visit in the extremely dark interior of the church a bad, scary scene took place. I had taken a picture (the one you just saw). That was when one of the guards came up, weaving slightly (you could smell the local Maya corn liquor or "huaro"). He said all photos were prohibited, and I truly had not realized it, flash yes, photos no. He and a couple of cohorts had just confiscated rolls of film from another of the tourists inside the same time as us. When I tried to explain (in Spanish) our good intentions, a drunken

Indian with a night stick approached me and demanded the camera and film. When I refused, he yelled "Silencio, este es un lugar sagrado, y ustedes turistas cabrones están bajo nuestra jurisdicción. Somos de la sagrada cofradía de San Julan Chamula."

He shoved, or better, herded Amy and me to a side door of the church, hustled us outside and made us stand against the church wall, calling for the outside guards to come and help him out. Once again, he demanded we hand over the cameras and any "bolsas" or knapsacks. We did but with me protesting in Spanish; his conversation with his comrades was totally in Maya. I pleaded our case, asking if I could see the "alcalde" or mayor of the town. At that point they pointed to a whitewashed tiled roof building to the side of the church, told us to go inside, and had us sit down on two very rough, hard wooden benches in front of a simple long table with chairs behind it.

In a few moments an elderly Maya man came in, dressed the same as the guards, but without "straw cowboy hat," a woven Indian shirt, black trousers and "personals" bag. He introduced himself as Tzotz, the local shaman and community leader; there was rapid conversation with our "guard" all in Tzotzil, then us with Tzotz in halting Spanish on both our parts. He reiterated the rule of no pictures in the church, "One of our last refuges from the 'ladinos' [whites] and foreigners," and demanded we take the film out of our cameras (which had been placed on the long table). Amy looked at me, nodded and said, "Don't do anything stupid. We are on their turf. And we above all should respect it." I asked if I could explain our presence in Mexico – seeing the major Pre – Columbian sites for my teaching of their cultures in classes in my far-off State of Nebraska (he wondered where that was), and that we would like to bring a few friends to see them (no mention of AT Travel). I assured him that we were in total agreement to protect the culture, the language, and the ways of his peoples. I mentioned my study and admiration for the "Protector of the Indians" Fray Bartolomé and of Bishop Ruíz. This seemed to strike a sympathetic chord. Tzotz, first said, "Words are cheap; believe me, we if anybody know that. As a teacher, which we highly respect in our culture, we can converse with you. There are still troubles here today. Originally there were some 50,000 to 300,000 Tzotziles in the area. My people are fiercely religious. As a result of a revolt by our ancestors in 1869 – may I explain - during our celebration of Holy Week we have a symbolic crucifixion and a local youth volunteers as our local "Crucified Christ" - many were arrested and taken prisoner by the government. The result: 13,000 of our people took up arms and killed many whites in the region. Some of our enemies took sides with the government.

"In more recent years many Indians have been expelled from our town for converting to Protestantism, that is, expulsed by us Chamuleños of the original true, local faith. The result: there are 30,000 Indians from our lands who now live on the outskirts of San Cristóbal, no longer dressing in traditional clothing and selling tourist articles to survive. They are trying to negotiate a return to their former lands. But we shall never forget our history and will defend it. That includes what may seem minor to you, the prohibition of cameras in our shrine.

"We have no expectations of any real justice from far off Mexico, D.F. or even from Tuxtla Gutiérrez, the capital of the 'ladinos.' Most of our lands have been lost to outsiders, 'ladino' white – faces mainly, but also to their allies, those of our former brothers converted to the new foreigners' Protestant religions. Bishop Ruíz is the one person who seems to be on our side."

"Señor Alcalde, sr. Tzotz, thank you for your patience and informing us of the situation. I respectfully tell you I took only one picture, and importantly with no worshipers facing the camera. They were kneeling in front of me, saying prayers and making offerings. I would like to at least make an offering to you, the church, for the right to that photo to show my students and countrymen the reverence and respect you hold in your native beliefs. I can arrange $100 as a token offering."

"Señor, I believe your words, the fact you are a professor and working to disseminate true knowledge of my people. Just this once we will make an exception, no more. I am reluctant to take your monetary offer, but can assure you it will be used well for the upkeep of the church."

I nudged Amy, we put our heads together and the last of our cash, amounting to $105 dollars, and gave it to the shaman. He thanked us and ordered the guard to usher us out of the town hall and back to our AT van. "Remember our agreement and see what you can do, even if in small ways, to help our people."

We bowed to him, shook hands and were marched to our van. There was one quick and hurried moment, I had to capture a ubiquitous Mexican scene – one of the local trucks parked in a lot next to the church and decorated from front to back with its driver's name and his perhaps girlfriend on the cab roof - "Josito and Lupita." Climbing quickly back into the van, we were soon back on the road to San Cristóbal, both breathing a sigh of relief, grateful to be safe, and mainly unhurt. The guards would not have been as kind as Tzotz. And in a humbling way to me, Amy reminded me to be a lot more careful when I got that camera out. AT and NYTT would not tolerate any such experience for their travelers! I said, "You are absolutely right. But appropriate arrangements can be made ahead of time, strict instructions to adventurers to avoid any problems." After arriving back to the hotel, we had a quick lunch and proceeded to the last thing on our list for this wonderful colonial town.

THE NA BLOM INSTITUTE

Na Blom Weaving of Bonampak

That p.m. we visited an important place, the "Casa-Hacienda de Na Balom" or "House of the Jaguar." Originally a Catholic seminary, today it is a museum, library and hostel for those researching the "Maya World." It was founded by a husband and wife, Franz and Trudy Blom. Today it is also known as the Na Blom Institute. Blom was an anthropologist who helped in the original excavation in the 1930s at Palenque and later with the Lacandones at Bonampak, the site with the most famous Mayan murals in all Mexico. The collection of "huipiles" and Indian dresses by Señora Blom is also among the best in Mexico. Both of our mouths watered for the wonderful woven carpet used as a bed covering depicting a famous scene from Bonampak. Amy said this place would definitely be on the "options" list for the town. The host at the museum told us if we wanted to see anything like the Na Blom "huipil" collection, there was a place in town, recently started (one year ago) that would be worth our while …

THE "COOPERATIVA DE INDIAS - HUIPILES"

Weaving Cooperative, San Cristóbal

So that p.m. there was a quick walk back to the market area of San Cristóbal and a visit to a "Cooperativa" of Indian ladies from the entire region. It was called "La Cooperativa o Colectiva Nna Jolobil de Textiles." The cooperative claims 3000 participating weavers from the Tzotziles and Tzeltales. Scholars say the designs on the weavings have as models the stelae-dinteles of Yaxchilán, a classic Maya site of one thousand years ago! (I showed the stela in our initial visit to the Anthropology Museum in Mexico City). Amy was gushing, thrilled, "I've never seen such a collection of authentic native art" and assured its addition on our list. The Maya ladies, both speaking fluent Spanish, were happy that we could send tourists and tourists with dollars in hand to visit their place. I asked the elderly lady where the notion came from for the pattern on her "huipil" [blouse]. She said, "It came to me as though in a dream."

When we got back to the hotel, there was Pablo Negrete, a smile on his face, "I heard of your 'adventure' in San Juan Chamula from the van driver. I'm glad you got through it okay. I would have come had you called me. However, even with my language facility, the mention of PF is anathema to these people. And for that matter they would have little love lost for Xolotl in DF, believing that most Indians have 'sold out' to the government – except them! And it may be true." Pablo agreed that our "donation" would be put to use, but maybe not in the church and it was a good compromise on our parts to get out of a bad situation. He said tourists have been beaten up, the town is officially "off limits" to San Cristóbal police and that only very delicate negotiations resolve such things. He wished us well on the continued trip saying that Palenque in his opinion is the foremost of all Pre – Columbian Sites in Mexico. "We have an agent in Palenque due to all the tourism and small-town crime in the town itself – pickpockets mainly. His name is Joaquim Guzmán and I'll tell him to get in touch with you. He will know where you are staying. Buen Viaje!"

Here we are again, a last night's dinner on a major stop of the itinerary! Where to go? You ask around town. Amy took charge and we ended up at a beautifully decorated place with "huipiles" on the walls, black and white photographs of the incredible façade of the Santo Domingo church, and paintings of no less than Diego Mazariegos and Fray Bartolomé de las Casas. The menu was pork and sauce, rice and flan, all accompanied by marimba music. I was in tourist heaven, remembering those early days in Guatemala (dancing with beautiful 'guatemaltecas' to marimba music at the Casa Contenta at Lake Atitlán), and may I say with a beautiful girl now at my side. Amy was very happy and relieved to be safe, well and soon to continue our journey.

Our talk: Amy was wondering what would be next in surprises. My stance was that San Juan Chamula really was an anomaly of sorts, a dumb tourist mistake on my part, and nothing related to the earlier business of Xolotl in Mexico City. Each place we visited seemed to outdo what we had just seen. Amy said adventurers and NYTT travelers, particularly the women, would wax enthusiastic over the Maya markets and all the weaving; it would have to receive careful but good coverage in the trip brochure. I insisted on a social note and a paragraph on local history to apprise adventurers of the tense social, political and even religious issues in

Chiapas, all in a way making for interesting travel. It was apparent things were indeed in a state of flux. We got out Amy's itinerary and the calendar and both could not believe we were more than one – half through the trip, day 12 of 20! My life – long dream of Palenque was about to come true; up to now it had been the intense study in Morley and Coe's books. We hoped to get an early start the next morning, get to our hotel in the town of Palenque and then out to the ruins in mid – afternoon. I learned they close at dusk.

We had that one last fire in the room fireplace at the hotel, got caught up on travel notes, and reminisced of the last two days. Both of us, barring any foreseen difficulties, were more than ever convinced my original idea of the itinerary and AT's and NYTT's avid support were correct and a good move.

10

TRAVEL TO PALENQUE, A SURPRISE VISIT TO "ÁGUA AZUL" AND SETTLING IN

After San Cristóbal, the road climbed and we were in thick pine country. At Ocosingo the road narrowed and there was fog and cold. We ate a snack of "galletas" and Fanta Naranjo for a van breakfast. From the pine forest we now entered into a very green, lush tropical forest with bananas etc. The hills were jagged, very like what we have seen in parts of Guatemala.

The Stop in Água Azul

Unbeknown to us, the van driver said there was something nearby we should not miss, the waters of Água Azul.

Mike and Amy and Agua Azul

After just a delightful hour spent at the waters; we chose not to swim but just look, the azure pools and falls "breathtaking." Our driver said it's just one hour to Palenque, "Vámonos pues!

PALENQUE

We arrived later that same day, finally, to the town of Palenque (not impressive, we would learn more later of its dire poverty) and to our very impressive hotel Misión Palenque just seven kilometers from the ruins with beautiful grounds, tropical flowers and parrots on the veranda in front of a long inviting swimming pool. We are in the lowlands and the climate is warm and humid, relieved with afternoon rains.

After our check – in at the main desk in the lobby in mid – afternoon there was supposed to be time to rest but we were both so excited we took our van at 2:15 to the ruins.

Once again for the trip plan and my subsequent letter to James Hansen of the "Times" – "What You Need to Know about Palenque."

Palenque is from the classic period 300 – 900 A.D. and is the site farthest to the west in the Maya area. It also was the first major classic site discovered. It is well preserved and noted for the beautiful architecture and sculpted lintels both in stone and stucco. It is considered the most beautiful site in Mexico (according to the local tourist brochure at the registration desk of the hotel) " … for the intimacy and relation between the buildings and the tropical forest. The sun light that passes through the morning fog is always special. One hears the sounds of tropical birds and even Howler Monkeys." It is considered the site with the most refined of American Pre-Colombian art. A chronology of Palenque is as follows:

1740. Antonio de Solís, a Spanish priest, discovers one of the walls of Palenque while digging in the soil in the planting of a crop.

1805. The first real expedition to the area takes place.

1832. A German count, Jean-Frederic Maxi Millen de Waldeck (an artist) lives with a lover for one year in the ruins in what we now call "The Count's Temple" in the North Grouping.

1840. This marks the arrival of Stephens and Catherwood to the site where they spend one year exploring the ruins and making drawings which will appear in "Incidents of Travel in Central America, Chiapas and Yucatán," a classic in the literature.

1923. The first "modern" expedition is conducted by Franz Blom.

1952. Alberto Rus of the National Museum of Anthropology discovers Pacal's Tomb!

Palenque represents the architectural height of the Mayas: there are works in stucco, ceramics and sculpted stone. There are no stelae or wooden ceiling "dinteles." The temples are of an architecture which is more sophisticated than that at Tikal or Copán: there are corridors within the buildings, subterranean stairways, galleries and forts in time of war. Much of this was done by the technique of building parallel, successive Maya arches.

The glyphs in Palenque were deciphered just a few years ago, an important moment for the study of Maya culture; 800 of 1000 glyphs are now deciphered.

The site comprises fifty square miles, and twenty-five per cent is excavated.

Another major difference from other Maya sites: the roof combs ("cresterías") are much more delicate in style.

Amy and I were both awestruck as we walked into the main entrance of Palenque Ruins, a well-kept meadow of grass with major buildings in front of us – the Palace ahead and to its right the Temple of the Inscriptions.

El Palacio, Palenque

Temple of the Inscriptions, Palenque

We went to the Temple of the Inscriptions first because it is indeed the most famous building in Palenque! It is seventy-five feet high and is a funerary monument to King Pacal, the first great king of Palenque.

After we climbed the steep stairway to the top level and its temple (a shaky Mike hanging on for dear life to the chain in the center of the steps; Amy heading up like, pardon me a local reference, a howler monkey), in the interior of the temple at the top of the outside stairway there are three sculpted panels with 617 blocks with glyphs, that is, Maya hieroglyphic writing. It is one of the Maya's largest inscriptions. My camera did not do it justice, too bad; I surmised because of the poor interior lighting, the years of wear and once again, not a really fine camera. The temple is built on nine levels, corresponding to the nine levels of the Maya "infra-world." From the tomb below to the upper gallery there are 13 corbelled arches which correspond to the 13 levels of the Maya heaven or upper world.

The main attraction is Pacal's Tomb. It is located 80 feet below the temple floor at the top of the pyramid. The story of its discovery, a rounded "plug" in the floor of the temple, by Mexican archeologist Rus in 1952 is one of the amazing stories of all Mesoamerican archeology. He was rummaging around the rubble in the temple and noticed a small round hole with a plug it. Upon closer inspection after sweeping the entire area, it revealed a cut stone that turned out to be the cover to a stairway. After getting the help of several strong assistants to lift the cover, Rus saw that the stairway was completely buried in rubble. That was the beginning of the formidable task of clearing what would be revealed as a stairway to the bottom of the pyramid. There was the tomb. Eighty feet down! The entire stairway was one of amazing feats of Maya architecture – a series of corbelled arches to the bottom.

Mike, Stairway to Pacal's Tomb

The tomb contained the remains of King Pacal together with jade objects and jewels (now removed to the museum in Mexico City). The sarcophagus is covered by a sculpted stone cover which depicts the deceased monarch falling into the jaws of the earth monster. Above Pacal's head is a mask that represents the "infraworld;" rising within it is a sacred Maya tree (the "Ceiba"), rising from the four corners of the world. The mask has a two-headed serpent, an image of the Maya heaven, and a quetzal bird at the top of the tree which represents the day sun at its zenith. The sides of the sarcophagus show ten persons coming out of the earth, beings that possibly represent some of Pacal's royal counselors. Pacal reigned for 28-38 years, dying in 692 A.D. He reigned possibly from the age of 12 to 40 or 50 years of age. All this was revealed by the literature on the site.

Pacal's Tomb

Even though I nor Amy had never seen the ruins of the Pharaohs in Egypt, and we are told they far surpass the Maya Civilization, this was a first for both of us. And even though we had seen a reproduction of the tomb in the museum in Mexico City, we were both a bit thunderstruck, awed but also a big frightened. Maybe because of the long, dripping wet slick stairway, and then the actual tomb only illuminated by one small electric bulb from a wire. We both wondered what in the hell was wrong with the managers of the site – this is not a small, unimportant Maya relic but one of its greatest discoveries and treasures. I tried to get pictures of it all, succeeded only partially, in part because one could not get elevation to really see the sarcophagus, so famous in itself. The carvings and images on the walls were still visible but of course the "cache" of jade, gold and Pacal's death mask had been removed to the museum in Mexico City.

We were alone in the room, maybe because it was late in the day, but for some reason were talking in a whisper. But after twenty minutes or so it was time to leave. I took Amy's hand and said, "I'm afraid this puts to shame that Anasazi stuff at Mesa Verde in Colorado. Take a good look. I'm hoping we can all come back. And the adventurers' cameras will do it justice. Maybe old Wonky will be along (he was notorious on the 'International Adventurer' for taking chances on photography.)

11

XOLOTL

It happened after we had spent perhaps thirty minutes in the tomb chamber. It was humid, the walls, floors were wet, it was hot, and like I said, for some reason, the only light was one of those old-fashioned single bulbs hanging from a cord. And strangely enough, no guards. You would think the site would have that as a priority, especially when the outside grounds were so well cared for. Weird, I thought. As Amy and I turned around to begin the climb back up those 80 slippery stone steps, there was a figure blocking the stairway. He was dressed simply, in loose white pants and shirt with a straw hat with a flat brim, sandals on feet. What made him different was the pistol in his hand pointed directly at us.

"Señor Miguel y Señorita Amy, por fin nos conhecemos! Hace tiempo que precisamos de una plática seria. Todo está planeado, como una de esas "giras" que uds. gringos hacen en nuestro México, pero yo soy su director y guía! Hay que subir la escalera, lentamente, hacia el templo arriba, y sin crear estorbos – en silencio. Yo los seguiré y arriba continuaremos nuestra 'gira.' Tengo dos amigos que nos esperan. Recuerden que soy yo quien tiene el revólver. Vamos, pues, uds. acaban de ver nuestro recinto más sagrado; espero que no lo vayan a olvidar."

I said, "Está bien, no somos burros y no vamos a crear problemas. Pero, quién eres? A quién debemos este encuentro."

"Después sabrán, sabrán todo. Ándales, pues."

We very carefully following instructions, climbed the dark, dimly lit stairway. Above there were two more men, both dressed like our captor (is that a good word?) He said, "We will all slowly go down the temple steps, like good tourists, I'll even point out some surroundings to you. At the bottom we'll turn left, walk across the clearing, and get into a blue van at the site entrance. I don't want to draw any attention so I'm not going to shoot you, but people often pass out going down these steps and my two friends are here to help us just in case."

We followed instructions, slowly climbing down (grabbing the chain in the center of the stairway and going down backwards), reached the bottom, walked to the van and were motioned in. The glass windows were darkened. Two men quickly put bandanas around our faces and told us to sit still and not make waves. The van was now crowded, me and Amy, and four of the captors. We drove slowly off, I think still on asphalted road for about 10 minutes, no one talking, and then on to a very bumpy dirt road. In about 15 minutes we pulled up to a stop, were ordered out, and then found ourselves in a very dark and smelly hut. The only light was through two windows and the doorway as we saw later. We were held by the arm and guided to two wooden chairs, but arms securely bound.

At that point they took off the blindfolds and we were found facing our original captor. "Pues, señores, hasta ahora todo bien. By the way we do not intend to harm you, but just have a serious talk for you to meet some 'real' Mexicans and perhaps learn of a new point of view. I can now answer your question, I am Xolotl, live normally in the environs of Mexico City, but move around a lot due to my duties for our political party, the DPN (Defensa del Patrimonio Nacional). We are extremely interested in your travels and research, mainly because they would bring another wave of ignorant gringos to our beautiful country, see our most sacred sites, and worst of all, tell all their friends what they've seen and urge them to come as well, a horde of unwanted visitors. We know all about you, your travel company AT and your co – partners the NYTT group. Señor Gaherty we also know your background and qualifications and congratulate you on them; after we talk you will understand why we think it best if you just return to your university after your current trip and just teach of our culture. Señorita Carrier, we cannot condone on the other hand any of your capitalist motivated work. Your companies may bring tourists and travelers and they may love what they see, but behind it all is the profit motive of your company and the results I've already talked about. We cannot allow your efforts to come to fruit."

I interrupted, but quietly, asking Xolotl if I could give some explanation and clarification to our research and planned trip, if there was any room at all for discussion or compromise (this was all in Spanish). Amy at this point had said nothing.

"Usted se atreve de hablar de 'compromiso' después de la historia de nuestros dois países! Ja ja. Pero, sí, te dejo hablar, como dije, no estamos aquí para dañarles sino educarles!

"Señor, I am correctly a 'gringo,' of Irish – American extraction. My ancestors faced prejudice in America for being 'foreigners' and Catholics. I think it is significant that I loved your official language (Spanish) and culture enough to dedicate my entire studies and life to it, and to Portuguese in Brazil. My primary concern in Mexico is two – fold: 1) the study of the popular 'corridos,' la voz del pueblo, and their contribution to Mexican music, folk poetry and history (I forgot art – José Guadalupe Posada and the 'calaveras') and 2) the Pre – Columbian heritage of your country which I have wholeheartedly taught and defended in university classes. This trip is not only to gather information for a possible expedition by AT and NYTT but MY OWN research and experience to many sites I have only studied and read about and never seen. These travels for me are a dream come true. I believe that an honest evaluation of your Pre – Columbian Culture and presentation of it to the world is only a positive. I defer to my colleague Amy to address your concerns to tourists and travelers to come."

"Está bien. La voz y la sabiduría de la mujer en mi cultura son muy respetadas. Suéltale la venda, déle una botella de água y escuchemos!"

Amy spoke, "Señor Xolotl, con todo respeto: Tambien dediqué muchos años al estudio del español, vivi un año en la Argentina, y aunque esté viendo esta grandeza de México por primera vez, Miguel podrá decirte como me ha impresionado y como aprecio todo. Ahora, sus dudas:

"La firma, 'Adventure Travel,' has more than twenty years' experience in maritime trips throughout the world. We have a sterling reputation for our generosity in payment of all fees, charges to governments, dock facilities and finally to local representatives, guides, drivers, and the like. I can vouch for this because I personally have written the checks. AT has brought over the years hundreds of thousands to the countries we visited.

"As for culture, our adventurers are inculcated with one principal concept: respect for the places and people we visit. Señor, as with honest diplomacy, it is person – to – person contact that makes for the peace and betterment of this world. If I can look you in the eye, speak with you, and see your point of view we are both better off. This in short is what we would bring to Mexico."

"Gracias a ambos uds. You have confirmed our belief and research on your persons. However, I posit to your memories:

Your invasion of Mexico in 1847 arriving as far as our capital of Mexico City, attacking our Military Academy and slaughtering many of the heroic youth of our country who defended it. The aftermath was our loss of the war to you.

What you call your "Manifest Destiny" causing the "Mexican – American" War of 1847 -1848 when we in Mexico in effect lost and ceded to you one   half of our national territory when overwhelmed by your military.

Your defense of the worse dictator our country ever saw, and enemy of the Indigenous peoples, Porfirio Díaz and the continued 'unofficial' support of right wingers who long have opposed our Revolution of 1910 and Constitution of 1917.

And the final insult, when you squeezed the last drop of Mexican territory out of us with the agreement of the "Chamizal" in Texas.

No less evil, I contest your thesis of economic good, at least in Mexico. The fees you pay never reach the common person, the capitalist owners and managers pocket it all; it amounts to just one more chapter in capitalist exploitation of our country and people. Where do your so − called rich "adventurers" stay? Only the luxury hotels whose management charges outrageous prices and incidentally gobbles up any tips to the poor workers in those hotels; in fact, your brochures say "tips" included. The same with the meals included. It is only the occasional "dinner on your own" when a cash tip may reach a poor Indian waiter's pocket. My political party and persons like myself have studied you and your colleagues for years. There is no doubt of what I say. And finally, most of your people, management and travelers, are abysmally ignorant of our country and people. The owners see the dollars to be made; the clients or adventurers as you call them, true, they are awed by the pyramids, the women love our weavings which they bargain for and never pay just prices, but they fear our food, our "turista" [Moctezuma's Revenge is actually not a bad term!], but enjoy and get drunk on our mescal, tequila and margaritas."

Both Amy and I could see the truth and the non − truth of Xolotl's arguments but it was not the time to make waves. I said, "What now Señor Xolotl? Oh, I have one question and something I don't understand: why the attack on Señor Roberto Reyes' office in Mexico City?"

"He, señor Miguel, is instrumental in a very large slice of what I have been talking about. Perhaps you can pass on to him the details of this conversation. I do not truly know if there is a remedy. Those in power in Mexico will welcome him and you and others like you. However, Amy you are right, when I hear you and Miguel, look you in the eyes, I am convinced this little 'break' in your tour and our conversation is the right thing. We will release you shortly, in fact give you a ride back to your hotel. I personally wish you continued good travel; we know your itinerary. Palenque awaits you and the Yucatan after that. I have one simple request: you conclude your travels, but you do not recommend this trip to your company. If we do not release you, the PF will come down on us and hard.

But we can tell you that as long as our Party and a few of us are breathing, future travelers are assured of experiencing some discomfort. Do I have your word on this?"

Amy and I looked at each other, I shrugged and said, "I'm actually glad we met you, had this talk and now are completely aware of your point of view. My love of Mexico and all its culture will never change, even taking into account this little 'aventura.' I can assure you that the 'grandeza' of your culture will always be taught truthfully in my classroom."

Xolotl looked at Amy and said, "Y usted señorita?"

Amy looked him in the eye and said (much to my surprise; this gal should have been a diplomat!): "I'd like to make a counter offer to you, this after hearing all you said. What if I talk to the management at both AT and NYTT and we institute a 'cash only' policy on all tips – hotel personnel, drivers, waiters, musicians and the like. It seems like a huge task, but it's not. Travelers can be forewarned and bring exact amounts of tips expected and in correct currency. This can be arranged so they are not in the streets with huge amounts of cash and victims of thieves. Secondly, if you can inform us of an honest entity (we also know the history of money and politics in Mexico) dedicated to the preservation of the Indigenous culture of Mexico, we can agree on significant donations to that entity after our trips."

"Words are cheap in Mexico, but I think you two are different. We will consider what you say and you will hear from us before you leave Mexico, probably at your hotel in Mérida. The fly in the ointment, as you say, is finding and determining an appropriate entity. I think another factor is concluding such an agreement with the dozens of other travel companies bringing the hordes to Mexico. Yours would surely constitute 'favored status' if you lead the way. On the other hand, believe it or not, there are others far more extreme and adamant than I in our movement. I will consult with them. Está bien. I am sure you are tired, hungry and would appreciate a nice bath, so we'll drop you off at the gate to the hotel. No one should follow us from those premises or there will be dire consequences. Un placer!"

We shook hands with Xolotl and his men and were escorted to the van. Blindfolded again, there must have been about a 30-minute drive, blindfolds were off and we were dropped on the road outside the hotel entrance.

12

◆━◆━◆

BREATHING A SIGH OF RELIEF AND WHAT NOW?

Grateful and worn by it all, we walked back to the room, reported at the desk we had a wonderful time at the ruins and intended to go back tomorrow, had those hot showers and dinner that night. It was delightful with rice, pasta, beef and tomatoes, chocolate cake and coffee. For me it was "down home food" and some of the best so far on our trip.

Conversation of course was subdued, private and trying to take in and get our heads around the day's developments. We shared not one but two bottles of French wine to settle our nerves. I told Amy, "I am so proud of you and I've never seen such courage and calmness by anyone, man or woman, under these circumstances. Amy, you are an amazing woman." She said, "You have no idea how I was trembling under those bonds on our hands. There are times when one says and does things as though they are guided by another force. That is what happened. Miguel, maybe there are guardian angels. I could say the same for you, and I will, Nebraska boy, this is turning into one helluva trip."

That night we managed to comfort each other in one of those twin beds in hotel rooms in Mexico, holding each other tight. Before sleep however we both agreed to go back to the ruins in the morning. No fear.

The next morning it was back to the ruins as early as we could get in the gate. When we first got there the weather was beautiful and came up to more than expectations from articles and books from National Geographic and documentary films and dreams over the years. It was dramatic, super green and all trimmed and in good shape. We trudged up the steps of the main palace.

El Palacio, Palenque

It is really a complex of buildings, 15 in all, built through several centuries. There are three large patios, galleries, all built on a platform 30 feet in height. In one corner of the Palace there is a three-story tower which perhaps represents the Maya universe. The Palace was constructed over a period of 200 years and six kingdoms. The columns of the galleries have stucco figures, for the most part representing Pacal and personages of his dynasty.

Stucco Image, Pacal's Foot

In the gallery of "Casa D" one sees a personage which represents the monarch with either a turned, twisted or deformed foot and a serpent of lightning-thunder. The evolved aspect of Maya construction is seen in the fact that the Palace was done placing one Maya arch parallel to another, thus creating interior space and more stable and strong walls.

The East Patio of the Palace

There are sculptures or "dinteles" of figures which are believed to be subservient, captives or the like.

An aside: human waste was handled at the Palace by the fact that the Rio Otulum was channeled to run through it, thus carrying off waters and materials. It runs between the Palace of the Inscriptions and the hill leading to …

The Palace of the Cross

Then we climbed up a terrace to the Plaza of the Foliated Cross and took in the scene. The Temple of the Foliated Cross is on a hill at the edge of the forest. The jungle was magnificent with birds and bird sounds, Howler Monkeys and we even spotted a beautiful Toucan. We just sat down, watched and listened. The preserved forest is the only reason these animals even exist. Amy and I both agreed that <u>this</u> was the place we had to get our naturalists if the trip were to come to pass.

There are two more temples in the complex:

The Temple of the Sun is the lowest, the first beyond the Río Otulum
The Temple of the Cross is the tallest

It is believed that this complex was done during the reign of King Chan Bahlum, 683 A.D., the son of Pacal. All three temples have parallel galleries, thus creating more space. Their stucco panels or "dinteles" show the birth of three patron deities of Palenque. My photo is imperfect but if you look carefully you can appreciate true Maya art.

Glyphs, Maya Art

Then it was "Home" to the hotel in the rain. We were thirsty and starved and excited for all we had just seen. There seemed to be no end to it. We had the big noon time meal with rice, pasta, beef and tomatoes, chocolate cake and coffee and an after-dinner Kalua. Incidentally, a small possum which roamed the beams above the dining room kept us entertained. This was our final scheduled day for Palenque and we had to "make tracks" as we say in Nebraska. Our final chance at these spectacular ruins.

Back to the Ruins.

We saw the North Group first, what we had missed or put down the list in the a.m. There are five buildings, the best preserved being the Temple of the Court (Waldeck the explorer was supposed to have lived an entire year with his lover here. My immediate reaction: they both should have got a bit moldy.)

125

The Ball Court

We discovered the only ball court on the site; I'll leave commentary on this major aspect of all Pre- Columbian to when we get to the best example on the trip, at Chichén – Itzá in the Yucatán. Suffice to say, like they experts say, there is always more to the eye that what is first revealed. The "game" was tied into religious beliefs, all very complex and with dire results. The ball courts are all different and each site has at least one. The most memorable for me was at Copán in Honduras, have to save that for later.

Then the rains came; it didn't matter. We had umbrellas and rain gear. Nothing could have torn us away from that unforgettable and who knows, once in a lifetime thrill, at least up to now. Well, maybe … Xolotl. It didn't happen.

So we bade goodbye to the ruins but promising we would come once again in the morning on our way to Villa Hermosa for one last look. That evening was magic, a wonderful candlelit dinner at the hotel, reminiscing what had happened the last two days, pondering the rest of the trip and plans. We never did make it to "downtown" Palenque but were assured we missed little; the good restaurants were all associated with the hotels out in the woods like ours. We jointly decided to put off any big decisions for AT and NYTT until the end of the trip, but would not hold anything back from either James Morrison or James Hansen. And we both agreed that Palenque was at the top of the Pre – Columbian list so far. There was even some time for some intimacy before crawling into bed.

The next morning after good café con leche, scrambled eggs and bacon, and orange juice, we packed the bags, put all into the van and headed to Palenque Ruins. I've included the original two views – the Palace and the Temple of the Inscriptions with an emotional Mike Gaherty saying goodbye.

The Two Palaces

There was one last note to add. After we left the ruins proper, we happened upon a really fine "artesanía" shop with finely done burned leather images of Pacal in all the classic Maya finery. There was painstaking detail both on the figure and dress of Pacal, but also on the reproduction of the glyphs. Amy knew about calligraphy in the Far East and said this was just as beautiful in its own way. This shop was for tourists to be sure (that is the only market for local artisans), but it was fine work, much like the leather maps we bought in Ipanema at the Hippie Fair on last year's "International Adventurer" trip.

Palenque was indeed a magnificent place, a magic place - the grandeur, the drama of the setting of the place, the forest, the birds, the monkeys, the temples, the carvings, the mist, and the river. A great spot.

13

THE SHOCK OF VILLA HERMOSA – THE RELIEF OF LA VENTA

Sad to be leaving Palenque, we began a two-hour van ride through green pastures and cattle country to Villa Hermosa. There were lots of Brahma cattle and cattle egrets, but alas, the mountains and forest of Palenque are gone! After that idyllic nature paradise of Chiapas we then faced the shock of oil rich modern Villa Hermosa. There were new trucks, Ram Chargers, clean, and modern. We then stopped at the VIPS Restaurant for lunch: "Buenos Días. Soy Carmita tu servidora." Right out of U.S.! I was now living on cough drops and ordered more chicken soup but dared to have a Negra Modelo to ease the pain.

PARQUE, MUSEO DE LA VENTA

Parque, Museo de la Venta

This museum outside of Villa Hermosa shows the best of the ancient Olmec civilization, predecessor to the Maya and other cultures of the Meseta Central in Mexico, the last of the so − called Proto − Cultures of Pre − Columbian Mexico. This culture was even earlier than Teotihuacán in Central Mexico but both are prototypes of the grandeur that would follow with the Classic Maya, the Zapotec, the Toltecs and the Aztecs. In the park one sees the famous Olmec carved stone heads, six feet high with "African features" and "helmets," each weighing twenty tons. There is a debate about what they actually represent: kings or queens of the old Olmecs? The facial features are similar to those of the present-day natives of Tabasco State.

There are many sculptures in the park; the famous Olmec heads, jaguars, priests, stelae, etc. They are from the sites of San Lorenzo, La Venta, Laguna de los Cerros and Tres Zapotes. We know these centers all had commerce to the west and south and an agricultural surplus due to the fertile soil in the Gulf Region. They were primarily ceremonial centers.

All the above represents a proto-culture of the area, that is, the earliest culture prior to the Maya. It was a culture that had the ball game, pyramids (small to be sure), sculpted portraits and a calendar and calendric system, i.e. mathematics. It was late in this era that the Maya calendars of 260 and 365 days were developed as well as the "long count." These "rudiments" of the later Classic Maya cannot be contested.

What caught our attention was a beautiful live but caged jaguar, among the most sacred of Maya animals. Amy and I were told of this magnificent creature back on the "International Adventurer" in Manaus, Brazil and had seen one in the zoo in Belém do Pará, but this one stunned us. It is unclear if the jaguar was actually associated with any specific Olmec or Maya god, but there is no doubt kings, queens, nobility and priests used the jaguar pelt or variations of it. It is most associated with the night.

Jaguar, La Venta

A not so serious aside: this Olmec Site with the huge carved heads and some carvings is located in Carlos Pellecer Park. We had seen such huge stone heads at the beginning of the trip in the Museum in Mexico City.

Rather than the atmosphere at Palenque, pardon me, it seemed more like a trip to the Zoo. My best photo, in fact, is the "Jaguar Movedor," short, swarthy, dark and powerful. Scary!

We now were at least 2/3 completed on the "gira." What was left would be no less spectacular, but representing the grandeur of Mesoamerica in a later and final phase. We boarded a flight on Mexicana the next morning to Mérida, the capital of Yucatan, an entirely different world from whence we came. The Pre – Columbian cultures and sites would be spectacular, but the city culture of Mérida would be different for good reason – its proximity to the Caribbean and especially to Cuba and its unexpected appreciation of France and things French.

14

INTRODUCTION TO THE YUCATAN

After a one hour wait in the airport of Villa Hermosa, we had a quick, smooth flight. As the Mexicana jet gradually lowered, we saw the Yucatán – mostly flat with a few low hills and then landed at Mérida. When we walked off the airplane into that inferno of heat and humidity both Amy and I longed for the greenness and coolness of the rain forest of Chiapas. We were in culture shock: our hotel the Holiday Inn is next to the Hyatt Regency, etc. It seemed more like Cancún. Amy said she did not have good lodging information before the trip but was determined to check out Mérida. Adventurers would otherwise experience the same shock. We would spend part of that morning at local travel agencies checking this out. It didn't take long; we moved the next day to the Mansión Mérida Hotel, just off the main plaza in a remodeled French mansion from the 19th century, more on that later.

Before I go on, as usual in my/ our trip report and my letter to Hansen of the "Times," here is what we need to know about the Yucatán. It's like another country!

THE ARCHEOLOGICAL ZONE OF THE YUCATAN

There is much to be told and clarified, a bit on the academic side I'm afraid, but necessary for the greater appreciation of it all. It reviews some of what we've seen, proposes some new and hopefully puts it all together.

I. Antecedents and History of the Maya Civilization in the Yucatán

1500 B.C. to 320 A.D. was the Pre-Classic Maya period in which Maya civilization developed with roots from the Olmecs or nomadic peoples in the lowlands of Guatemala. It is in this period that corn or maize came to dominate agriculture and give it stability.

From 500 B.C. to 320 A.D. the Maya calendar was developed as well as hieroglyphic writing, ancient Maya architecture and a religion with 166 deities. Much of this was in the Olmec area, in Kaminaljuyu in Guatemala and the developing sites to be seen in the Classic Period.

The Classic Period, from 320 A.D. to 925 A.D. was seen in Palenque in Mexico; I hope we can figure out something to include the other great sites not in Mexico: Copán, Quiriguá and Tikal.

The above Classic sites outside the Yucatán were abandoned around 800 to 900 A.D.

There was a migration between 900 A.D. and 1200 A.D. of peoples from Guatemala and Chiapas to the peninsula of Yucatán and Campeche, "an inferior copy of the previous grandeur" according to one scholar! To be debated!

The Maya Puuc Style of architecture and culture became established in the low hills in the west of the Yucatán, in sites like Kabah, Sayil, Labná and later, Uxmal. Note that Uxmal was contemporary to Chichén-Itzá and was founded by a Mayan people, the Tutul Xiú.

The Putún people were what was left of the Mayas (perhaps of Mexican origin) and they combined with the Toltecs from the Valley of Mexico to dominate the Yucatán peninsula.

These invaders (Putún and Toltec) came to be known as the "Itzáes" and had as their legendary leader the god-man Quetzalcóatl. They were the people that constructed "new" Chichén and later on Mayapán.

There came to be a sort of pacific Confederation between Chichén-Itzá, Mayapán and Uxmal until 1194 when the people of Mayapán (the Cocom) defeated the Confederation, sacked Chichén-Itzá, conquered Uxmal and captured the leaders of the Itzá and the Xiú.

The Xiú took vengeance in 1441 when they attacked Mayapán, destroyed it and its Cocom leaders. They then founded a new center called Maní. From this time on there was constant warfare until the arrival of the Spaniards in the 16th century.

The Arrival and Conquest by the Spaniards

The conquest took only twenty years to accomplish. The Spanish "adelantado," Montejo el Viejo, left Spain in 1527 with 400 soldiers. He arrived first to Cozumel Island, then to Xel Ha on Terra Firme. Battles with the natives and other difficulties forced him to abandon the east coast and head west where he tried to establish himself again, this time in Tabasco in 1530. He failed again due to the resistance of the natives, and by the way, there was little gold found, to the dismay of the Spaniards. At this time news arrived of the Spaniards' success in Peru and the huge amounts of gold and silver found there, so little attention was given by the Crown to Montejo's cause.

Then in 1540 Montejo once again established himself in Campeche, then Mérida in 1542, and in the entire peninsula in 1546. The chief of the Xiú people offered himself as a vassal or subject to Montejo, was baptized and took the Christian name of Francisco Montejo Xiú and allied himself to the Spaniards to defeat the Cocom.

After the conquest the native peoples were decimated by war, sickness and slavery. This is the epoch of Fray Diego de Landa, Bishop of Yucatán, who studied and wrote of the Maya but also destroyed their books of hieroglyphic writing and art - the "codices." Only three remain.

Yucatán was governed by decree from Spain and not from Nueva España (Mexico). With Mexican Independence in 1821, the governor of Yucatán resigned, and Yucatán was declared to be an independent country. This only lasted for two years.

The Nineteenth Century

This was the period of the development of the huge henequen (jute) and sugar cane plantations; the Indians remaining were deployed as slaves and the "company store" system was installed: "la barraca." The result was that the Indians became completely financially indebted to the whites. But they also served in the Army of the Yucatán, thus obtaining the arms necessary for a large rebellion in 1847. But a few people got filthy rich.

The War of the Castes 1847. The Indians attacked and massacred whites in Valladolid, buying their arms from the English in Belize. Until June of 1848 they controlled the Peninsula except for Mérida and Campeche. Overconfident from victories, they left the war suddenly to plant the spring corn crop. In the interval, fresh troops arrived from Mexico and massacred the Mayas, some of them fleeing to distant jungles in Quintana Roo.

The "Talking Crosses" refers to an Indigenous cult in the southern part of Quintana Roo around 1850. Responsible was a Maya ventriloquist and also a Mestizo priest who incited the natives to rebel against whites and kill them; this in the town of Santa Cruz. The battle continued to 1866 when a truce was arranged.

By the end of the 19th century new federal troops from Mexico with more sophisticated arms arrived and took the rebel territory. Thus, finally there was an end to the War of the Castes.

TRAVEL IN YUCATÁN

Amy and I were exhausted, and all in all we admitted the comfort of the Holiday Inn was indeed a respite that first night. The move the next morning however to the restored 19th century French Mansion just off the main plaza was welcome, all modernized with air conditioning and soundproofed for the street noise right outside in the plaza. It's like we jumped forward one hundred years from the Misión Palenque or the "chiminea" of our hotel room in San Cristóbal de las Casas. The first outing still in the a.m. was to the nearby Plaza Montejo. You have to watch the time of day, do nothing during the heat of the day, and use the evening when the heat meliorates. The beautiful stone carvings of the façade of the Montejo Palace are impressive but reveal much upon closer inspection.

Palacio Montejo, Mérida

La Casa de Montejo. Father and son together conquered the Yucatán and founded Mérida in 1542. The Palace was constructed ten years later in 1552 in the architectural style of the Plateresque and was remodeled in the French style during the age of the boom of henequen or "sisal." The original columns of the façade show the conquistadors walking or standing on the heads of the "bárbaros" or barbarians. We were amazed that had not been "disappeared" but Mexico never ceases to amaze. Our "friend" Xolotl would not have been pleased; there is an entire ugly chapter of the Spanish and the Catholic Church in Yucatán. One of the famous bishops did an unforgivable thing – he ordered the remaining Maya "codices" [books in hieroglyphic writing] to be destroyed as offensive to the "true religion." This was Fray Diego de Landa in 1562. The amazing contradiction was he himself was responsible for one of the best and most complete books on the Maya in Yucatán – "Relación de las Cosas de Yucatán," the account of Maya society just before the arrival of the Montejos and the conquest of the same place. Only three codices survived and are in Dresden, Paris and Madrid. He called them "Superstition and Lies of the Devil." Ahem … the devil is in the details – he burned them all.

The main avenue of Mérida the Paseo de Montejo was inspired by the French boulevards, in this case the Champs – Elysée. It became can I say a "phobia" of the henequen (jute) millionaires of Mérida to travel to France and in effect become "frenchified" (somewhat akin to the "afrancesados" in Spain in the early 19th century when Napoleon invaded and Borbones came to rule). This tourism took place at the end of the 19th century, a bit of a conundrum – Mexico as a country spent several years in war to kick the usurper French out! Yucatán never really went along with Benito Juárez and the "Restoration" from the French. We walked to the "Gran Glorieta" on the Paseo with its modern sculpture of Pre-Columbian Mexico. The "Monumento de la Patria" on the Montejo Paseo is in what they call a "Neo-Maya" style, done in the 1950s. It was unlike anything we had seen so far in Mexico.

One of the few places that was air – conditioned or at least had good ceiling fans was the Municipal "Opera House." It was there in the p.m. we enjoyed in the Palace a concert of old Yucatecan Music – two guitars and voice and one zither of 155 strings - "el harpa de Salomón." The performance reminded of Trio Los Panchos, but with songs from Colombia, Cuba and Yucatan composers. This was Yucatecan music!

Musicians, Mérida

Oh, it was Sunday. Once more the two cradle Catholics returned to their roots (I daresay after some discussion and debate). We ended that p.m. in mass at the Mérida Cathedral jammed with locals; the good news was we saw several Indian ladies in woven Yucatecan "huipiles." The bad news - a windy priest. Then it was people – watching time later at a quiet plaza near the church with a huge la Ceiba shade tree: Montejo León beers and pizza. It was pleasant to hear some mariachi music; there were few foreigners, a locals Sunday crowd in Mérida.

This was followed by a fine dinner at Amy's request in our hotel's restaurant specializing in international dishes, among them French cuisine. Okay. That was the appetizer, not the main course – that remained for Uxmal and environs for the next day.

15

TO UXMAL

The next morning we were well fortified by the breakfast meal at the hotel - "omelete de huevos, queso, jamón, jugo de naranja, piña, melón, y chocolate." Then it was to our van (once again with a driver set up through old friend Roberto Maya in Mexico City) and the ride to Uxmal.

Background for Uxmal

It is an "elegant" Maya site in the Yucatán from the 7th to the 9th centuries A.D. Uxmal represents the "Renaissance" of late classic Maya culture, but now in the Yucatán. There is still mystery shrouding its peoples, but in general it is thought they had migrated from the lowlands of Guatemala and Mexico when those sites declined. (You may wonder why; it is one of the major questions debated yet today among Maya scholars; long term drought, interurban warfare.) Uxmal is contemporary to the last days of Tikal and Palenque and is the best example of Puuc Maya Architecture: fine sculpted mosaics in relief in stone, friezes on the upper parts of facades, intricate cornices with "masks" with large "noses," – called "Chacs" and referring to the rain god of the Yucatán; rows of columns and high Maya arches. Its lines are clear, simple and "classic" to the point that the Governor's Palace has been compared to Greek classic temples!

The Highlights of Uxmal. Like good local Rotarians we "did" the entire site and were amazed at one building or area after the other.

The "Magician's Pyramid," ("Pirámide del Adivino")

Pyramid of the Magician, Uxmal

Stairway, Pyramid of the Magician, Uxmal

At 125 feet it is the highest edifice of Uxmal. Thus you see it from afar in the flat terrain of the Yucatan. Of elliptic (oval) design, constructed on four previous pyramids, it has a stairway with a giant Chac mask, the local rain god with an open mouth and a large stone nose. On the west side, on the top, there is a temple in the Chenes style (a style prior to the Puuc). On the opposite east side there is a sculpture which represents a king of Uxmal coming out of the mouth of a serpent. Serpents and feathered serpents are ubiquitous in the Yucatán.

One of its legends: a dwarf who was born from an egg built the pyramid in one night, thus its name "The Pyramid of the Magician." It is built entirely in a clean and simple style which represents a king of Uxmal, once again, coming out of the mouth of a serpent.

The Nuns' Quadrangle ("El Cuadrángulo de las Monjas")

The name comes from early visitors who were reminded of a nuns' cloister when they saw it. It has 70 rooms, and one side has large serpents on its wall. There are Chac masks on each cornice, and there are Maya huts ("chozas") on another wall. The latter are called "Na" in Maya; perhaps we remember "Na Blom" [House of the Jaguars] Institute in San Cristóbal de las Casas. The patio of the quadrangle measures 76-61 meters wide. By the way, if you have been listening (or reading from the "Letters" to Hansen) the similarity to the stonework of Mitla near Oaxaca and Monte Albán is a bit startling.

The Nuns' Quadrangle, Chac Masks, Huts

There is a Classic Maya Arch (and classic tourists) leading from the Nunnery to the rest of the site. At a nearby much smaller place, literally a crossroads in the Yucatán, one sees a huge arch like this with a stone – paved road on either side. The "sacbés" were at one time all over the peninsula.

The Governor's Palace ("El Palacio del Gobernador")

The Governor's Palace

This is the crown jewel of Uxmal, and one of the jewels of all Pre-Colombian sites in Mesoamerica. It dates from the 9th and 10th centuries A.D., is 1000 meters long, 12 meters deep and 8.6 meters high. There are 13 doors giving access to 20 inside rooms. The decoration of the front façade is in mosaic with a total of some 20,000 sculpted stone blocks (according to one local source, once again the coincidence or not with Mitla). There are also Chac (Rain God) masks, and the entrance "doors" are formed by the classic Maya half-arch. It is considered by one archeologist as "the most significant building of the Americas" (Victor von Hagen). In the central door there is an effigy of an enthroned king with a background of two-headed serpents and with other dignitaries to the side. The building is oriented to the East in order to see the morning star

(Venus; remember Quetzalcóatl – Kukulcán, the feathered serpent first left Mexico for the east, possibly converted into Venus the morning star, and then returned, an entire other story. Moctezuma the Aztec leader suspected the blond Cortés to be the reincarnation, or so it is said). It was, perhaps, a large administrative building (this is conjectured, but possible). It provided lodging for Stephens and Catherwood in 1841 and was first excavated by Franz Blom (of San Cristóbal de las Casas' fame).

The GOK Pile ("God Only Knows") – Reassembly of the Site. If you have ever wondered at the massive amount of work of the archeologists, anthropologists and most important, the local native labor, to reconstruct all the sites of Pre – Columbian Mesoamerica, this single photo at Uxmal gives a hint.

The GOK Pile

Amy and I would conclude that long visit to Uxmal with a return to the tallest building but to its back side – the large pyramid of the Magician or "Adivino."

A DISCLAIMER FOR AT, NYTT AND THE "LETTER" TO JAMES HANSEN

Now is as good a time as any. There are several good reasons why I do not delve more in Amy and my trip's diary - narrative into what is seen and its possible meaning. The first is that I do not have the credentials to do so, i.e. archeologist or anthropologist specializing in Meso-America. What I do possess, and told AT and NYTT prior to their agreeing to sponsor my and Amy's trip, is a sense of curiosity and admiration for all that we have seen, but probably more directed to the visual captured in the hundreds of slides I took. During graduate school I enthusiastically read anything I could get my hands on pertaining to the topic, i.e. classic books and especially any articles from National Geographic Magazine. But I found that sometimes the more I read, the "less" I knew, always recalling the statement of a scholar whose name I do not recall, "With the Maya, all is always more than it seems." But as a result of all this reading I also discovered an important thing: the experts themselves do not agree on the meaning of much of the Maya world, and one constantly notices the words "perhaps, possibly, maybe" and the like in their own narratives when referring to concepts, buildings, images and decorative objects. No doubt the deciphering of most of the Maya glyphs in recent decades has aided immeasurably in knowing some things "for certain," but even then, the experts admit that "much is to be done." I liken the whole thing, a bit, to religion and the existence of god: it cannot be proved, but as Joseph Campbell said, "Where would that leave 'faith'?" Thus, it is the "mystery" of much of the Pre-Colombian Civilizations that in fact fascinates me. So be it.

All this applies at Chichén – Itzá, but pardon me, "piled higher and deeper." The mix of very late classic Maya, but in the Yucatán, and the influence of the Toltec migration from Tula complicates the matter even more. Amy and I intentionally leave it for last.

16

CHICHÉN - ITZÁ

We traveled from Mérida to Chichén on yet another day by the AT van at 8:00 a.m. It was two hours to the ruins; the site was literally jammed with tour buses and groups, mainly from Mérida and the Yucatán Coast. Upon my suggestion, we followed history, thus the old Mayan part, and then the Toltec-Mayan part and the "cenote" [sacred well].

Here is my usual blurb to AT and NYTT and the "Letter" to James Hansen.

Background on Chichén-Itzá

The name means "The Mouth of the Well of the Itzáes." It was a post-classic Maya city absorbed by the Toltecs who had migrated from central Mexico around 987 A.D. Legend has it that they were led by their leader-chief, the legendary Quetzalcóatl (known as Kukulcán by the Mayas) who arrived from the west to "redeem" his people. The same Toltecs abandoned the city of Chichén-Itzá in 1224 A.D. It is not clear what was the exact relationship between the Toltec people and the Itzá people (late classic Mayas) or even the Xiú people (late Maya); it is all debated. But what is clear is that the Toltecs-Itzáes built many new edifices which were added to the old Maya site of Puuc Style (contemporary with Uxmal). Toltec motifs such as the plumed serpent, warrior columns, jaguars and eagles, chacmooles, and skull racks all came in this later phase. Our description of the site obeys this original chronology; therefore, we note the old Maya part and then the newer Toltec-Itzáe part.

We first entered the original old Maya part. The first major edifice is called the "Caracol" or Maya "Observatory."

The Maya "Caracol," Chichén – Itzá

The Maya "Caracol"

The building is in the Maya Puuc style: it is a round edifice built on top of a quadrangular platform, with an interior stairway in the form of a snail or "caracol" climbing to a high tower. On one side it is decorated with Chac masks, the Maya rain god in the Puuc style. There are narrow, vertical windows in the round building, and it is believed that from them one could see the cardinal directions, the Spring and Fall Equinoxes, and the Summer Solstice. The theory of the windows is based on the supposed observation of the Morning Star of Venus.

An aside: it is curious to notice that among the Aztecs, centuries later, the temples dedicated to Quetzalcóatl, in his identification with Venus the

Morning Star, were always round. We remembered the case of the temple dedicated to him in the "Plaza Mayor" next to the "Templo Mayor" in Tenochtitlán.

The Nuns' Convent and the Iglesia. Chichén

The Nuns' Convent or the Annex of Maya Chenes style is highly decorated with Chac masks (remember: Maya rain god) and serpents with a "king" in the center. The building called the "church" or "Iglesia" is two stories or floors with Chac masks and representations of an armadillo, a crab, a snail and a small turtle. All are Maya spirits called "bacab" which are believed to sustain the heavens.

You do not have to be an expert to see all the similarities to Uxmal. We both formed rather strong opinions on the two sites, old Maya and newer Toltec – Maya.

THE NEW CHICHÉN

The Temple of the Warriors

The Temple of the Warriors

This main edifice has a group of the 1000 columns (of Tula – Toltec style). On the top platform one sees the figure of a Chac Mool, a reclining warrior in front of sculpted columns with the figure of the plumed serpent, and the serpent heads (one on each side) as in the temple of Quetzalcóatl at Teotihuacán in Central Mexico. On the columns one sees low relief warriors in the style of Tula (Toltec).

In the rear part of the Temple of the Warriors the building seems to almost take on "Greek or Roman" characteristics. The figures in the middle of the wall represent Quetzalcóatl, the plumed serpent (always associated with Teotihuacán and Tula in regard to the good, but here representing Venus, the Morning Star). One notes that in the jaws of the serpent (earth monster?) there is a human head surrounded by eagle feathers. A personal query: is this the god – man Quetzalcóatl coming into life? (This is also in the Puuc style as at Uxmal. As I've written and hinted, the plumed serpent was ubiquitous in all Mexican Mesoamerica.)

Temple of the Jaguars.

There are columns with serpent heads and sculpted panels of jaguars. Originally, inside, there was a fresco depicting a battle between Mayas and Toltecs.

The Ball Court (one of nine at Chichén)

I emphasize the ball court with two images because it is so large, so impressive.

The Ball Court

The Carved Warriors, the Ball Court

This ball court is the largest at Chichén, in fact the largest in Mesoamerica, and also the best preserved. They used a ball of hard rubber and apparently tried to pass it through one of the two rings on either side of the court (the ring is a stone sculpture of a rattlesnake). On the walls of the sides of the court, vertical walls, there are sculptures which represent opposing teams. In the middle sculptures, there is a scene in which "death" accepts the sacrifice done one surmises by the winning "captain:" the head of the losing captain! The winner has the head in one hand, an obsidian knife in the other.

Amongst all the thousands of pages written on this, the fact and the speculation, it is clear that it was more than a "game," and was tied into religion, the movement of the stars, moon and sun. That's all I'll say. Maya ball courts we have seen are similar, but this is a huge subject, I'm not an expert. The most beautiful I know of is not in Mexico, but at the wonderful Maya site of Copán in Honduras, hopefully a topic for another AT trip.

Temple of the "Tzompantli"

The Temple of the Tzompantli

The heads of the victims of sacrifice were cut off and placed on posts, side to side. This "templo" represents the deed; there are also eagles which devour the hearts of the sacrificed. The word "Tzompantli" is of Toltec, not Maya, design. The same type of temple exists both in Teotihuacán and the Plaza Mayor in Mexico City. The story: human sacrifice, probably in the Toltec – Aztec sense, to provide sacred blood to nourish the sun god in his efforts to conquer the night and bring each new day. You can tell it was all getting to us by maybe this not so funny photo. Even professors and their girlfriends get weary.

The Sacred Well of Chichén-Itzá

I did not get a decent picture, but you walk down this road or "sacbé" to the pool of the sacred well - "El Cenote de los Itzáes." There is evidence that victims were thrown into the well, women and children among them (as told by their bones), perhaps of "abnormales" or people with physical defects, deformed or even mentally deficient. Once again stories and books abound, excavation done by hand with divers, "loot" carted off by tomb robbers. I haven't really talked about the latter but it is a scourge in all Mesoamerica, the most famous anecdote, that modern robbers have developed a chain saw that can cut through the stone of the Maya stelae, cut them in halves or thirds and cart them out of the ruins on mules or horses.

Thompson, the American Consul at the beginning of the 20th century, actually "bought" the Hacienda de Chichén, that is, the entire site, and with the machinery of the times dredged the bottom of the well and found bones, gold, jade and the golden sphere or plaques which depicted the sacrifice scenes. All is found today in the Peabody Museum at Harvard.

The Great Pyramid or "El Castillo"

The Castillo – the Great Pyramid

I've saved the best or at least the largest for last. The downside, the Castillo is mobbed by tourists, Amy and I among them. They say you have to go very early in the day before all the tour buses arrive from Cancún, or late in the p.m. This is what we knew about it in our "homework" before actually getting there:

The pyramid is Toltec-Mayan. This is the pyramid the scholars relate to the two Maya calendars. It is 75 feet high with 364 steps (91 on each side), and a platform step. There are 52 panels on each side, matching the 52-year cycle of the Maya. There are nine terraces on two sides of the pyramid, thus a total of 18, the number of months of the Maya calendar. Is all this conjecture? I have to trust the experts who did the counting. On March 21st of each year one sees the spring equinox. As the sun sets, for a period of 34 minutes, one sees "the serpent of light" which seems to descend to earth, from top to the bottom of the pyramid, culminating in the serpents' heads. The day and the solstice event represent a "Symbol of fertility of the Mayas," the sun "enters" mother earth, and all know that it is time to plant the corn. And the hundreds or even thousands of tourists feel closer to … the divine?

The famous, huge tall Castillo is built upon another temple, and there is a tunnel-stairway inside the old temple. For some reason we withstood the first inclination to climb the outside stairway like hundreds of others, but then decided no, let's do the interior stairway first. We entered the humid, hot tunnel - stairway with dozens of other tourists and both of us were fighting real claustrophobia (natural I think in the circumstances) and shortness of breath until arriving after what seemed forever to the top. The occasional bare bulb tiny light did not help; the lights blinked several times. At the top of the stairway is a room with a "throne" in the form of a jaguar, of cinnabar color, with jade eyes, and a Chac Mool Altar. The old Maya often used the figure of the jaguar in this way. The room is small, the jaguar stone in the middle. I don't think we stayed long. Chichén provided no guard, no guide, unthinkable in shrines in most of the world. It was only later we realized the room's importance and what we had seen. I suffered shortness of breath, a rarity for me, was sweating profusely when we reached the bottom of the stairway and almost ran to fresh air. There were lines of tourists cramming each side of the tunnel – stairway while we were in it. You may imagine the odor; I'm amazed no one passed out around us. Was this smart? I do not know. We were told to wait awhile until tourist buses began to leave in early afternoon (to avoid the heat) and the crowds would thin out for the climb to the top of the "Castillo" as the Spaniards named this pyramid.

Mike and the Stairway of the Castillo

What remained was the "new" temple on top of the pyramid. After all the days of our research trip, and the marvelous scenes, this was to be the last. (An ironic understatement.) Maybe I mentioned or not, Mike Gaherty evidently has a fear of heights. Amy Carrier on the other hand is a regular mountain goat. The people who run all these archeological sites figure on people like me, so for most of the tall pyramids there is a heavy-weight chain in the middle of the stairway to hang on to get to the top. (The case at Teotihuacán, Palenque and Uxmal previously for us.) So on this very hot day in August, a water bottle and camera tucked into my Indian woolen shoulder bag (better than a pack) from Guatemala, we began the climb, Amy first and way ahead of me, up higher. I'm taking it easy, following someone's instructions to not look to the side or for sure to the rear. I'm not kidding. As soon as I reached that magic top level, I crawled on my knees to the temple wall, put my back against it and breathed a sigh of relief. I was not actually dizzy but, let's say, a bit unstable. Amy coached, saying just take a few deep breaths, breathe out slowly, and close your eyes if you need to. That seemed to work.

After just a few minutes I was able to stand and with Amy beside me, walk around to the entrance of the temple where you can see the bas- relief images carved and painted over 1200 years ago! I'm afraid my level of concentration was not too good. There were tourists there, and you had to watch out for the Type A folks in a hurry. But we said this is not to be hurried and walked around to the side facing the East and the Sacbé to the Sacred Well and the Temple of the Warriors far below. I was still shaky and had to sit down. Then things got strange.

Amy and I were contemplating that incredible scene, water bottles in hand, photos taken, marveling at the people, the culture, and mainly the whys and wherefores of this amazing place on earth. Other tourists had begun the climb down the stairway, the afternoon moving on. Then a shadow and then a figure came around that narrow passageway from the other side of the temple and stood to our side, and began talking rapidly to us in Spanish. He was dressed in that rural Mexican peasant outfit, loose white cotton pants and shirt and straw hat. He said we should have a talk.

"Señor Gaherty y Señorita Carrier, it is a pleasure to have your acquaintance at this perhaps our most sacred monument – you have already noticed the Feathered Serpents at the base of the wall before you, Kukulcán or Quetzalcóatl – our god of the truth, of the good, he who provided corn to our peoples and he who will bring us all to our ultimate glory with him. In your case sooner than later.

"I am a colleague of Xolotl whom you have already met. He has discussed with me and others of our Party for the Defense of the Patrimony of Mexico your tentative commercial agreement. So I know he plans to meet you in Mérida with our collective decision as to your research and time in Mexico. However, I personally think there is really very little to discuss at this juncture. Look around you – dozens of tour buses with their exhaust and huge tires making a parking lot of Chichén, women in scanty clothing, and mobs of ignorant foreigners desecrating this holy place. They take pictures, develop them and put them in a drawer, forgetting forever what we have allowed them to see. Suffice to say, I believe if our cause is truly to be noticed and believed there must be an example for all to see. You do not need to talk in Mérida. You can go to your death knowing that your blood sacrifice has indeed played a role far beyond any tourism - nourishing Huitzilopochtli the Sun God's trip across the sky and the return of Quetzalcóatl. Please stand up, both of you!

We noticed at that point that he had a very long, menacing knife in his hand, and it was black (Jesus! I thought! It's obsidian like the knives of the old priests used in Aztec sacrifice). We both managed to get up, our backs pressed against the temple wall, just maybe three or four feet from the edge. I said, "Can we at least discuss this?" It happened in an instant – he moved toward me (Amy was just to my side) along that narrow stone floor; I moved toward the man with my hand on the woolen travel bag with my camera and water bottle inside. As he started to bring the knife to stab me in the chest, I swung the bag at him, the knife grazed my arm making a six-inch gash, but I pushed him away, he teetered just slightly, and that was enough for Amy to grab his ankle and pull. He tripped and then tried to regain his footing and I pushed him again.

The dozens of tourists still at the base of the pyramid heard the scream all the way to the bottom. He literally tumbled down the 9 levels of the huge edifice and landed face down at the bottom, the body bloodied and doubled up with smashed bones between the two large feathered serpent stones.

The Feathered Serpents, The Castillo

There were screams, a mad rush of people, and then Mexican police. Several then looked up, noticed us, and yelled "No se muevan! No se muevan! Estarán presos en poco tiempo."

I think about five uniformed police were already scrambling up the main stairway and then to the top. I yelled, "Solo nos defendimos! El hombre abajo en ropa blanca tenía una navaja de obsidio y amenazó a matarnos! Diré todo a Jaime Torres de la PF de D.F. Él nos conocerá."

"Está bien, pero por ahora, vamos todos a bajarnos lentamente por la escalera. Nuestros colegas les esperan abajo. Ni piensen en correr o escapar." (In retrospect that was indeed a Mexican understatement!)

I hugged Amy, both of us with tears in our eyes. "You saved our lives Amy. My god what I've put you through."

"Mike, I think <u>both</u> of us saved our lives. But it sure is getting dicey traveling with you. I think we better get to the stairway, you first, gringo medroso!"

I managed to climb down, face to the stairs, still afraid to look in back of me or to the side. Amy had my travel bag and I worked my way down just holding on with the one good hand. My left arm was a mess, bleeding profusely. At the bottom a uniformed "policía" had his pistol trained on me, waiting for Amy to make it down. The others joined him and then there was a cloud of dust and a blue van with PF on the side roared up. The officer in charge said we would be taken to the main police station outside the ruins with first aid equipment there to temporarily patch me up. That happened, a large white bandage covering my arm when they were done, and they gave me a shot of something and that made me woozy.

The magic words must have been "Jaime Torres," because the officer said, "We've already put in a call to headquarters in the D.F., and Jaime Torres got on the line. He profusely apologizes to you, but says he will get a flight immediately to Mérida where he will meet you this evening. We were guided into another van and given an escort, no sirens noted, to a "Pronto Socorro" in Mérida.

We were told later what had happened at the scene. The police just in those few hectic moments after the incident had to confiscate several cameras from tourists or maybe the Press at the base of the pyramid and the Feathered Serpent stones. They formed a small cordon around the cadaver. Soon an ambulance arrived, men with a stretcher put the cadaver in a grey bag into the back of the van. The police closed the site with barriers along both entrances. A cleanup crew (the blood and torn bits of clothing) would assure there was no sign of the incident. Officer Pedro (the first policeman who had yelled at us and eased us down the stairway) told us they found the obsidian knife halfway up the terraces of the pyramid on the fourth level. There was no word yet on the attacker.

Two hours later in Mérida a Doctor cleaned my wound, bandaged it and said careful washing and salve the next three or four days should fix me up, but wanted me to get it checked in the interim. He checked Amy as well, but other than the shock of it all, she seemed to be okay. We asked permission to go to our hotel, take long hot baths to clean up and relax, and what the hell, get something to eat. It was granted, they once again gave us a ride but this time in an unmarked car. All very hush – hush. After the baths and food, now about seven p.m., the phone rang and it was Jaime Torres requesting a meeting. He said he was in plain clothes as a precaution, maybe we could meet in our room which had a living room attached.

A few minutes later we were face to face with Jaime. It turned out to be a long talk. After assuring him we both we okay, he requested a blow – by – blow account of our being assaulted on top of perhaps Mexico's most famous pyramid. After that he said, "We work fast when we have to here in 'mañana land.' (A small joke.) Your attacker, may he rest in peace, was indeed a colleague of Xolotl in the DPN Party, but they were not great friends. He makes Xolotl look like an upstanding citizen! His name was Tadeo Garófalo, he with one – fourth indigenous blood, probably Zapotec, and had an arrest record as long as your arm. Petty theft (pick pocketing), and assault with a deadly weapon (that obsidian knife or a small revolver), primarily of tourists in Mexico City. "It is very easy there to pull a quick street robbery and fade into the crowds." He had served time in the D.F. Penitentiary for such crimes on two occasions but was released in months the first time, and one year later for the second.

"He is, or rather, was, I think you say in your parlance, 'a loose cannon.' A virulent indigenous nationalist, a voting and fringe member of the DPN Party, but disavowed by their leadership, even including Xolotl. They see and saw him as truly "unbalanced" and did not want any association with him. What I can tell you is that you shall suffer no more from him or anyone like him. We will have a plainclothes guard near you every step you take until you leave Mexico. I know this infringes on your privacy, but as guests in our country doing the type of research you do, and particularly taking into mind today's incident, you really have no choice. Mike and Amy, I do not know if you realize how close you came to death, but we at PF are damned sure it won't happen again. I do respectfully request knowledge of your remaining plans. I understand the Yucatan was to be your last stop. And just as important as your personal safety, I want you to know as a representative of the PF and our link to the National Tourist Board, we do not want you to cancel plans for AT and NYTT. Tourism is too important and valuable to our country. And we are proud of what we have to offer."

Amy spoke first, nudging my arm, "Señor Torres, thank you for all you have said and done for us. Mike and I have not talked; there has really been no time, of even tomorrow. In just a few days Mike is due to return home to his teaching at the university, I am due to be back to my regular job in September, "safe" on a ship in the ocean, working for AT. All either of us can do is file our research report with the management of AT and NYTT; theirs is the final decision on whether to proceed or table it all. I have to say honestly that in spite of your good efforts, we did not exactly receive the protection I at least thought we would get after our initial meeting in Mexico City.

"It has been a secret thus far, but at this point you need to know what happened to us in Palenque, in the depths of that temple at Pacal's tomb and later."

I interrupted Amy, "Amy, we have to respect the terms of that agreement, but now with today's event, I agree with you and think we have to share that experience with Señor Jaime and take his advice as to what to do. Do you agree?"

"Yes, but with reservations. Xolotl said he would be in touch with us in Mérida with the Party's decision, and I'm sure by now he will be totally aware of the attack in Chichén. I can't predict what he will say or do. You better fill officer Torres in but Jaime you must promise to keep this secret, close to the vest as it were, because I'm not going to feel safe otherwise."

I nodded to Jaime, he nodded back, so I in effect took the next fifteen minutes to tell the entire episode of Xolotl in Palenque, the kidnapping, the several hours as prisoners, the talk. (Jaime said, "Don't spare any details. We need to know all this.") "Like Amy, I don't know how he will react to today, if he'll disappear from sight, or more likely, surprise us and put us into a tight and dangerous spot again. We know he is capable of violence but hell he seemed even with his extreme opinions to be rational and we made great progress in understanding each other and really established some trust. There was in effect an agreement. But he was the one who said he would reestablish contact."

I was thirsty, so was Amy and Jaime even said, "A cold beer might be acceptable under the circumstances." I ordered a six pack of icy Dos Equis and a bottle of French wine for Amy, it arrived shortly, and we came up with a plan, uh, of sorts, Jaime of course taking the lead.

"Coño! (pardon my serious Mexican swear word), but you have got my attention. Our man in Palenque never notified us of any problem with you, and that's strange. He was assigned to keep track of you and to come to assistance if need be. He will be receiving a phone call from me shortly. Be that as it may, we are sitting here now with a problem and decisions to make. I have a visceral reaction to all this, but I need to know what precisely was the 'agreement' with Xolotl?"

"Señor Jaime, I think your man in Palenque may not have known of our brief kidnapping, and if he did, decided to not make waves fearing for violence to us. He would have had a chance to contact us, after all, that last day at the ruins before we left for Villa Hermosa. Secondly, as far as we know, Xolotl is keeping his end of the bargain. We cannot reveal to you the terms of the bargain for I am certain Xolotl would react violently to that, but I can say that it was rational and even diplomatic. We don't know if Xolotl had any contact with this attacker today, but I think we have to take a gamble and see if he does contact us. We are due to fly out tomorrow mid – afternoon to Mexico City, spend the night, and fly back to Los Angeles the following morning. Shall we take a chance and see if we hear from him? I for one, and I think Amy will agree with me, believe that unless there is some resolution from Xolotl we cannot proceed with any future plans for AT or NYTT."

Jaime reacted, "But we cannot let him or the DPN dictate terms either. We will keep plainclothes guards near you, believe me, until you depart from Mexico. I'll be at the airport tomorrow and we'll figure out a joint plan then. And if Xolotl contacts you, you will be 'tailed' so that's all I can do right now. Está bien?"

We agreed, what else could we do? Jaime apologized once again and left us. I confess to drinking the rest of the Dos Equis and Amy the wine. You don't get stabbed at the top of "El Castillo" every day. We even laughed at that a bit. As the alcohol set in some we both tumbled into bed and were out like a light.

Things evolved the next morning including some surprises. Outside the hotel room there was a copy of the local newspaper. A two – inch headline in "La Prensa," Mérida's main newspaper had two pictures under it – one of our attacker lying crumpled at the base of the "Castillo," the other a blurry picture of Amy and me surrounded by police at the other stairway. The headline:

Two Tourists Attacked on Top of the 'Castillo'
The Attacker Dead, Identities of Tourists Withheld by Federal Police.

There's no need to quote the story verbatim because it had no further information. It did express someone's reaction (the editor?) - "The scandal, outrage and sorrow Meridians and all Mexicans should feel that visitors to one of Mexico's major archeological sites, both a source of income to our country and a symbol of good will between Mexico and the world, should suffer attack and possible death." The outrage was directed first of all at the security police of Chichén and secondarily to the State and the National Police. "We are awaiting a quick response from law enforcement officials. Like it or not, tourism is our 'bread and butter,' and news of such incidents will surely and quickly affect this national industry."

Like I said, the photo of me and Amy was blurry, so we surmised we would not be an item of attention out in the streets of Mérida. After all there are literally hundreds of such tourist couples in the city each day. Then the phone rang, I picked it up and a familiar but slightly muffled voice said, "Señor Michael y Señorita Amy, cumplo con mis compromisos. Please go to the plaza in front of hotel, find a seat at one of the tables at the outdoor café, order a drink, and I will find you. Te veo en 30 minutos." I hesitated, looked at Amy, she nodded, and I stammered an agreement to the request.

We both had time to think, what of our safety? Jaime had assured us we would be closely watched by the PF, so we figured that would be the case. After quickly dressing we proceeded out the door, down the corridor and out the main door of the lobby of the hotel to the plaza. We had been to that outdoor café just two days ago, so found a spot under the huge shade tree, ordered coffee and waited, on pins and needles I may say.

In what must have been thirty minutes a man approached us, dressed in tourist attire, a light blue "guayabera," neat, white, creased linen slacks and white dress shoes and a rakish Yucatecan straw hat. He sat down, now without the mustache and his hair dyed a light brown. But no doubt it was Xolotl. We bade him sit down, ordered another "café con leche" and some "churros" and proceeded to have this tense conversation. He went first.

"Miguel y Amy, estoy a par de todo lo que ha pasado, inclusive con el contacto de la PF. They I am sure are watching us right now. First of all, I want to say sincerely that I am sorry for what happened with Tadeo and the fact you were truly put in danger of death. He was a renegade in our movement, distrusted and even hated by many. I am truly sorry it came to this. Miguel, I see your arm is bandaged, but it looks like a professional job, and Amy you look beautiful as always. This conversation has to be short, and I am counting on you to ameliorate any nasty business should the PF appear. They know me well and I have even had an occasion or two to meet sr. Jaime Torres, not always pleasant to be sure. If they try to arrest me, I have a weapon and all this will not end well. I think they realize that. I request time for a slow, methodical withdrawal for me without police interference; you may have to assure that.

"Down to business; I have talked at length to the highest officials in our Political Party and our cause. We perhaps surprisingly enough have concluded to give your proposal a try with a temporary trial. Our past opposition to foreign tourism and its ugly consequences has come to nothing. It can be very simple as we agreed in Palenque: all fees, tips, gratuities and other incidentals to our citizens who should encounter and serve your travelers will be paid directly to each person in cash in the future. Secondly, we do have an organization that will gladly accept your fees, I should say 'donations,' to our cause. It is called "Movimiento Nacional Indígena de Seguro Social," is located in Mexico City and has a sterling reputation, using your own words Amy, for its honesty. We will expect a check for each trip you sponsor in Mexico of 10 per cent of the gross cost of each traveler. This arrangement shall last for one calendar year. Your company and NYTT will be publicized for their cooperation and pioneer efforts in such matters. In other words, other companies will be highly encouraged to join your efforts or may see, let us say, a lack of cooperation in the granting of tourist cards or visas. In Mexico we are famous for what you call the "mordida," or as some of you disparagingly call it, the 'bribe.' But if you are Mexican and expect the wheels of daily life to turn readily, we simply call it a 'fee' or 'endorsement.' Are we in agreement?"

Amy spoke, "Señor Xolotl, this is more than we could have possibly asked or expected. As I said, all we can do is present it to our managers and await their decision. But it sounds fair and fair for all of us. How do we contact you?"

Xolotl produced a business card with the address of the 'Movimiento' and said mailing address and phone numbers are current. He said, "This may represent a real 'diplomatic' breakthrough and be an honest effort in repairing the past. The word is 'confianza' or trust; there is only one chance and one year. Please convey my regards to your people, and to Señor Jaime." He stood, shook our hands, and disappeared at the other side of the Plaza.

Five minutes had not gone by until Jaime Torres himself came to the table. "We heard it all; that fellow two tables away had amplification in his jacket pocket. If Xolotl had pulled a gun he would be dead now. So it seems the plan is thrust upon us; we at PF will wait until hearing from you and then see what to do. If your plan for the AT and NYTT trip proceeds with due permissions we will sit tight with continued surveillance of the DPN and Señor Xolotl. We would do that anyway. You will have undercover guards to the airport, on the plane to Mexico City, to your hotel, and then tomorrow until your departure for Los Angeles. Mike and Amy, I'm glad you are safe, and Amy, you in particular have paved the way to resolve this problem. My congratulations! If you ever need another job, we will find a place for you at DF or the Tourism Department. Mike, your study, knowledge and quick thinking have also brought all this to fruition. We hope to see you in a year or two with your travelers."

"Gracias, Jaime. We both need rest now. If you will excuse us, we'd just like to go back to the room and rest." He agreed; we went back and did not only rest but collapsed. Before that however, I had a brainstorm. After all we had been through maybe we needed a real rest, how about Cancún? And we could see if that place might serve for an extension to the AT – NYTT trip. Amy did not need convincing.

I called Jaime Torres the next morning and we had a brief conversation. I thanked Jaime for everything, but I added, "Sr. Torres, Amy and I had a bit of a brainstorm as we were resting last night at the hotel. As you may be familiar with customary tourist trips, there often is a paid extension. In this case we think there is an excellent possibility – Cancún, its beautiful beaches and water, and on down the coast to Tulúm. Amy and I would like to check that out, a matter I think of three days. If all pans out as we surmise, we would add it to the tentative trip. After our three days, as planned, we would return to Mexico City, tie up loose ends and then fly home to Los Angeles."

Jaime said it was an excellent idea, so on we went.

Mérida the Next Day

That afternoon, both of us refreshed after the stress and strain of the preceding day we took our last AT van ride with AT who whisked us to the Mérida airport for a very quick one-hour flight to Cancún. Our goal was to relax in that incredible clear blue water, maybe just lie in a hammock with a good book, enjoy some margaritas and Mexican sea food. And check out the possibilities of a post – trip add – on for AT and NYTT after the big trip to Mexico. We had correctly surmised that the Guatemala and Copán ruins and affiliated cities would have to be a separate trip.

Mike in Cancún

Amy had called the Fiesta Americana in Cancún from Mérida, brand new and one of the first tourist hotels in the frenzy of building of what the government called "the new and improved Acapulco." Remember it's just the beginning of what the government thinks will be a massive "boom" on the Yucatan Caribbean coast. There was some reason for the change: Acapulco was getting a bit stodgy in 1973 (its peak was really in the 1940s, 1950s and mid – 1960s). Although still a big tourist attraction both for Mexicans and foreigners, in all honesty it could not match the incredible sky – blue waters of the Caribbean. Nor the snorkeling and scuba diving which were top – notch and there was the proximity to the Maya ruins of the Yucatan – picturesque Tulúm on the coast and of course Chichén – Itzá and Uxmal near Mérida.

Our hunches all turned out to be correct. The margaritas were terrific (it was the time of Jimmy Buffett's "Margaritaville"), the shrimp terrific and (am I allowed to say) the terrific American fast food we ordered to the room. (Uh oh. Three "terrifics.") We had a wonderful view of the blue – turquoise water from our 6th floor room, sat by the pool in deck chairs and read and Amy splurged with a hotel massage at the very edge of the ocean. Tomorrow will be the tourist "schtick" – a visit to Tulúm.

Los Voladores, [The Flyers] Cancún

We witnessed the daredevil Tabasco Indians doing the ritual, with some trepidation I daresay. Pardon me, but it seemed to be the east coast's version of the divers at Acapulco. Maybe not. All went well on this unexpected event on the way to Tulúm the next day.

Mike, Amy, Tulúm

We did take a tour to in my mind the one remaining Pre – Columbian site close by – the small and rather insignificant ruins of Tulúm (with the tourists and iguanas) but with its amazing setting on a bluff high above the ocean. And a great swim in the surf and white sand. It was actually a historic spot - the first Spanish explorer Juan de Grijalva sailing along the coast in 1518, coming from Santo Domingo and Cuba (this was before the conquest of Mexico by Cortés and the Yucatan by Montejo) must have seen the small pyramids of Tulúm.

We then figured a three – day extension for AT would do it. After Tulum Amy walked and taxied me up and down the beach in Cancun to the half dozen completed hotels and to three separate Mexican "fine dining" restaurants.

What else? We are not night clubbers and besides did not want to join the rowdy teenagers and college kids and tourists that seemed to populate the area, so we enjoyed those sunsets and sunrises for two nights, and mainly caught up on our Mexico notes, observations and the plans for AT in Los Angeles and James Hansen in New York.

And there was time for what I would call "intimacy," getting to know more of each other's lives over long talks in the room. We really seemed to mesh, in all ways, and talked of how we could make a pretty good team in the future. First on the trip to Pre – Columbian Mexico should it come to pass, then back on "International Adventurer" to Brazil in 1976, and then, it seemed far away, to the ports of Spain and Portugal in 1977. We both figured that by that time we would either have a plan for Amy to become a faculty wife from September to May (gulp!) and both of us AT staffers in the summers. Or not. Uh, we said we'd figure it out later. Ha. The next morning we would do the return to Mexico City.

The Flight to Mexico City

With a long sleeve guayabera over me (hiding the bandage on the arm) and all packed it was uneventful to the airport. We managed the bags, the waiting room and 30-minute delay and then found ourselves on Mexicana and soon seeing the volcanoes around Mexico City.

Popocatépetl and Ixtaccihuatl

Alberto in his AT Van picked us up and whisked us once again to the María Isabel. There would be a short meeting with Roberto Maya the next morning at 11:00 a.m. and then a 2 p.m. flight direct to Los Angeles.

I think we were exhausted and perhaps still living those moments at Chichén – Itzá. We were still "shell – shocked" from the close escape on the pyramid. There was time for two strong drinks; we said to hell with the exorbitant hotel price of real scotch in Mexico and in a luxury hotel and had two Glenlivits apiece. We held each other close, hugged and kissed, and admitted we were glad to be alive. I don't think it registered until that moment how terrifying it was on top of that pyramid. I said, "Amy, you know I'm terrified enough just of the height and never would have made it up there without that chain in the stairway. Much less what happened later."

Amy said, "I won't say you did something stupid slamming his arm with just your tourist bag with the camera and water bottle. I guess we'll never know."

"Amy, you saw his eyes as well as me and that knife in his hand. He was not thinking of any 'nice talk' and wanting to discuss archeology. I'm just grateful you were not taking a siesta and were able to grab that ankle. Do we have to confess this when we get back home to mass and a priest? I don't think so, but I will anyway. It seems just like yesterday, but I don't think we will ever forget it." I kissed her again; we were quiet for just a moment and she said, "'Stand by your Man,' Tammy Wynett says, and laughed. Or is it sit by your man and don't grab the wrong ankle!"

"Amy, there may be a deeper meaning. Not any real malarkey about God taking care of us, but a sure sign we are indeed together, for better or worse!"

"Is that some kind of a Gaherty proposal? If it is, down on your knees!"

"Not exactly, sorry, besides you cannot hold me to anything right now. Remember, we are in shock. I'll just say, it's food for thought. Maybe it was a guardian angel or a whole passel of them or my protector St. Michael. I just want to tell you I'd rather not be with anyone else than you!"

"I'll take a rain check on the rest. Come here sweetheart!"

Amy said later, "Hey Mike, there's one more French restaurant here in Mexico City I've got to check out for AT before we leave. Can you take real French champagne, escargot, shrimp in wine sauce, and maybe a truffle sprinkled over it? It's on me and AT. You my afraid of heights professor have earned it."

"We both have. Amy these weeks have been the most exciting and happy of my life. … Uh, so far."

So we hopped a taxi to someplace with a name I can't understand or pronounce, Amy dealt with the menu and the manners (it was still bilingual – French and Spanish) and we had a last great dinner in Mexico City. We talked of the last weeks, all that we had seen and all that happened, and were still both positive our idea was a good one. We would sleep on it, talk again on the flight home to Los Angeles and decide what to tell James Morrison and James Hansen.

The next and final morning in Mexico City. When we arrived at his small office on Insurgentes, Roberto Maya had a big smile saying he was so grateful we were okay, congratulated both of us and kidded Amy that he would rather be dealing with her from the "International Adventurer" ship to shore phone coming in to Acapulco or Vera Cruz. A lot easier on the nerves. His business was back and running, even humming, the "incident" at Chichén – Itzá duly noted (he had been filled in by Jaime Torres; big news all over Mexico, and had seen the Mérida newspaper article). He suspected there would be no further trouble or contact with Xolotl in view of the agreement which he heralded as true progress for tourism in Mexico. We promised to communicate any decision after our meetings in Los Angeles.

Lots of Mexican "abrazos" ensued and we said goodbye.

17

---·◆·◆·◆·---

LOS ANGELES, DECISION TIME AND LIFE GOES ON

Alberto took us directly to the airport, there was a quick review by customs, and the wait went quickly. Soon we were comfortable in business class for the four-hour flight to Los Angeles. I held Amy's hand while we toasted each other with the complimentary champagne, and it must have hit us quickly; we both were exhausted and slept for perhaps two hours before the smog at LA International.

The taxi wove through Los Angeles traffic to the Marriott. We checked in and spent the rest of the day organizing our trip notes, photos and deciding what we would tell James Morrison and James Hansen. After our initial talk, Mr. Morrison would get on the phone, a conference call, and the three of us would talk to James Hansen in New York. Amy and I reviewed the entire trip, each giving our favorites, and less favorites, seeing if we would eliminate places for the trip report and recommendation. I had done such extensive homework on the Pre – Columbian sites and accompanying cultural "musts" so that nothing really could be eliminated. Most of the work was Amy's in regard to final recommendations on hotels and restaurants. What remained was the number one question: the DPN political party, the Xolotl business, the attack at the pyramid, and what do we recommend.

The next morning much rested and fortified with a good breakfast and coffee, we were off in a taxi to AT. A big hug from Susan Gillian and then we were ushered into James Morrison's office for the big confab. There's really no need to report on the verbatim. James and Susan of course were relieved we were safe and sound, and James initially expressed serious reservations about the whole thing. Amy more than I defended the trip and particularly the agreement with Xolotl and the really positive changes it could potentially bring to tourism in Mexico, a win − win situation for all. AT could lead the way for other travel companies and in a sense be first in line for future tourism business. James's eyes lit up a bit on that and said "Let's give it a whirl." That was what we presented to a skeptical James Hansen in New York. Amy's reasoning and my enthusiasm won them over! It was decided to forge ahead with the initial plans for the trip for the summer of 1975. That would mean advertising would begin this Fall of 1973. We were congratulated on the good work, and for surviving what came up. Goodbyes were made after a dinner that evening once again at Chasen's. Good food, good drink, and friendships forged. James reminded me that "Around Brazil on the 'International Adventurer'" was being advertised and scheduled for summer, 1976. What remained was my decision as to Portugal and Spain on "International Adventurer" with Harry Downing (and Amy) for 1977. I would have to think about the latter, see about research for preparation and let him know soon no later than Spring, 1974.

EPILOGUE

After returning to work, I at the University in Lincoln and Amy on the ships for AT, she and I received a registered air mail letter which we forwarded to James Morrison at AT and James Hansen at NYTT. The letter was from Roberto Mayo in Mexico City (translated from the Spanish).

September 4, 1973. Dear Amy and Mike, I thought you would like to know the latest from here in the office in Mexico City, news and updates from your previous escapades this summer. There was a very small article printed in "Excelsior" from the 'Official Daily' the congressional report no one reads in Mexico. It was dated yesterday.

The Mexican National Congress passed yesterday an unprecedented bill, this because it was sponsored by a minority party the DPN, Defense of the National Patrimony. It received unanimous support in the legislature. The law requires all foreign tour companies operating in Mexico to follow the rules stated below:

All foreign travel companies henceforth from January 1, 1974 will abide by the following rule: all tips, gratuities and such spent by the foreign companies and their patrons, including their agents, guides, drivers and wait personnel shall be paid in cash, either U.S. dollars or in Mexican pesos. There will be no exceptions. And furthermore, such companies will pay at the end of scheduled trips a ten (10) per cent fee based on the cost of each travelers' tour fee in Mexico, this to the "Movimiento Nacional Indígena de Seguro Social." The Congress recognizes the initiative of

Adventure Travel and New York Times Travel as pioneers in this effort. There will be a trial period of one calendar year; based on results, a decision will be made to either extend or amend this rule.

Mike and Amy, I guess you have to be careful what you ask for; only time will tell how this works out. The idea is that the "Movimiento" will distribute such fees to the respective Indigenous entities in Mexico according to each travel region. The law also stipulates full and timely reports from the "Movimiento." There will certainly be another level of paper work, but I surmise your companies will see positive results in upcoming bookings this fall and next spring.

Jaime Torres has informed me that, guess who, Xolotl (real name Alejandro Gomez) has been granted a full pardon for past minor criminal activities and in effect put on parole watch. He said the PF will be closely watching your old friend! I think we shall all benefit, but it does remain to be seen. We shall keep you posted and look forward to your tour next Summer.

I called Amy right away, and she returned the call, ship to shore, from near Lisbon. She personally was overjoyed, me a bit more skeptical. We decided to meeting during Christmas vacation to celebrate and renew our "friendship." I bought a ring, something different, a beautiful Brazilian tourmaline in a gold setting, and brought it with me to our encounter in Denver.

ABOUT THE AUTHOR

Mark Curran is a retired professor from Arizona State University where he worked from 1968 to 2011. He taught Spanish and Portuguese and their respective cultures. His research specialty was Brazil and its "popular literature in verse" or the "Literatura de Cordel," and he has published many articles in research reviews and now some sixteen books related to the "Cordel" in Brazil, the United States and Spain. Other books done during retirement are of either an autobiographic nature – "The Farm" or "Coming of Age with the Jesuits" - or reflect classes taught at ASU on Luso-Brazilian Civilization, Latin American Civilization or Spanish Civilization. The latter are in the series "Stories I Told My Students:" books on Brazil, Colombia, Guatemala, Mexico, Portugal and Spain. "Letters from Brazil I, II, and III" is an experiment combining reporting and fiction. "A Professor Takes to the Sea I and II" is a chronicle of a retirement adventure with Lindblad Expeditions - National Geographic Explorer. "Rural Odyssey – Living Can Be Dangerous" is "The Farm" largely made fiction. "A Rural Odyssey II – Abilene – Digging Deeper" is a continuation of "Rural Odyssey," "Around Brazil on the 'International Traveler' – A Fictional Panegyric" tells of an expedition in better and happier times in Brazil. And now, the author presents a continued expedition in fiction: "Pre – Columbian Mexico – Plans, Pitfalls, and Perils."

Published Books

A Literatura de Cordel. Brasil. 1973

Jorge Amado e a Literatura de Cordel. Brasil. 1981

A Presença de Rodolfo Coelho Cavalcante na Moderna Literatura de Cordel. Brasil. 1987

La Literatura de Cordel – Antología Bilingüe – Español y Portugués. España. 1990

Cuíca de Santo Amaro Poeta-Repórter da Bahia. Brasil. 1991

História do Brasil em Cordel. Brasil. 1998

Cuíca de Santo Amaro – Controvérsia no Cordel. Brasil. 2000

Brazil's Folk-Popular Poetry – "a Literatura de Cordel" – a Bilingual Anthology in English and Portuguese. USA. 2010

The Farm – Growing Up in Abilene, Kansas, in the 1940s and the 1950s. USA. 2010

Retrato do Brasil em Cordel. Brasil. 2011

Coming of Age with the Jesuits. USA. 2012

Peripécias de um Pesquisador "Gringo" no Brasil nos Anos 1960 ou "À Cata de Cordel" USA. 2012

Adventures of a 'Gringo' Researcher in Brazil in the 1960s or In Search of Cordel. USA. 2012

A Trip to Colombia – Highlights of Its Spanish Colonial Heritage. USA. 2013

Travel, Research and Teaching in Guatemala and Mexico – In Quest of the Pre-Columbian Heritage

  Volume I – Guatemala. 2013
  Volume II – Mexico. USA. 2013

A Portrait of Brazil in the Twentieth Century – The Universe of the "Literatura de Cordel." USA. 2013

Fifty Years of Research on Brazil – A Photographic Journey. USA. 2013

Relembrando - A Velha Literatura de Cordel e a Voz dos Poetas. USA. 2014

Aconteceu no Brasil – Crônicas de um Pesquisador Norte Americano no Brasil II, USA. 2015

It Happened in Brazil – Chronicles of a North American Researcher in Brazil II. USA, 2015

Diário de um Pesquisador Norte-Americano no Brasil III. USA, 2016

Diary of a North American Researcher in Brazil III. USA, 2016

Letters from Brazil. A Cultural-Historical Narrative Made Fiction. USA 2017.

A Professor Takes to the Sea – Learning the Ropes on the National Geographic Explorer.

  Volume I, "Epic South America" 2013 USA, 2018.
  Volume II, 2014 and "Atlantic Odyssey 108" 2016, USA, 2018

Letters from Brazil II – Research, Romance and Dark Days Ahead. USA, 2019.

A Rural Odyssey – Living Can Be Dangerous. USA, 2019.

Letters from Brazil III – From Glad Times to Sad Times. USA, 2019.

A Rural Odyssey II – Abilene – Digging Deeper. USA, 2020

Around Brazil on the "International Traveler" – A Fictional Panegyric, USA, 2020

Pre – Columbian Mexico – Plans, Pitfalls, and Perils, USA 2020

Professor Curran lives in Mesa, Arizona, and spends part of the year in Colorado. He is married to Keah Runshang Curran and they have one daughter Kathleen who lives in Albuquerque, New Mexico, married to teacher Courtney Hinman in 2018. Her documentary film "Greening the Revolution" was presented most recently in the Sonoma Film Festival in California, this after other festivals in Milan, Italy and New York City. Katie was named best female director in the Oaxaca Film Festival in Mexico.

The author's e-mail address is: profmark@asu.edu
His website address is: www.currancordelconnection.com

Printed in the United States
By Bookmasters